THE DUKE'S DILEMMA

Luella Hanley's father dies while they are in Milan and after the funeral she goes to the Cathedral to pray.

Alone and penniless she knows she must ask the British Embassy for help. But she feels it is humiliating to have to do so.

Sitting in the aisle she watches a marriage ceremony taking place in one of the chapels.

The bride and bridegroom sign the marriage register and leave the Cathedral.

It is then Luella notices a priest acting rather strangely. He pores over the marriage register, and when the two servers come back to take it away, nearly knocks them over in his hurry to leave.

Outside in the sunshine, Luella decides to make her way to the British Embassy.

Then a middle-aged, fatherly man asks her if she is alone and seems very concerned when she says she is.

She tells him where she is going and he insists on escorting her there.

On the way he has another idea and invites her to come with him to his office to discuss a proposition which might interest her.

While she is there the priest whom she noticed in the Cathedral bursts into the room.

How Luella realises she is in danger. How she agrees to take a little Italian boy to his father in England. How she meets a Duke and presents him with an appalling dilemma is all told in this sinister, but romantic 503rd novel by Barbara Cartland.

THE DUKE'S DILEMMA

by

Barbara Cartland

This first world edition published in Great Britain 1994 by
SEVERN HOUSE PUBLISHERS LTD of
9-15 High Street, Sutton, Surrey SM1 1DF.
This title first published in the USA 1993 by
SEVERN HOUSE PUBLISHERS INC of
425 Park Avenue, New York, NY 10022.

British Library Cataloguing in Publication Data
Cartland, Barbara, *1902–*
  Duke's Dilemma.
  I. Title
  823.912 [F]

ISBN 0-7278-4559-4

Typeset by Hewer Text Composition Services, Edinburgh.
Printed and bound in Great Britain by
Redwood Books, Trowbridge, Wiltshire.

ABOUT THE AUTHOR

Barbara Cartland, the world's most famous romantic novelist, who is also an historian, playwright, lecturer, political speaker and television personality, has now written over 581 books and sold over 600 million copies all over the world.

She has also had many historical works published and has written four autobiographies as well as the biographies of her mother and that of her brother, Ronald Cartland, who was the first Member of Parliament to be killed in the last war. This book has a preface by Sir Winston Churchill and has just been published with an introduction by the late Sir Arthur Bryant.

Love at the Helm, a novel written with the help and inspiration of the late Earl Mountbatten of Burma, great uncle of His Royal Highness The Prince of Wales, is being sold for the Mountbatten Memorial Trust.

She has broken the world record for the last eighteen years by writing an average of twenty-three books a year. In the *Guinness Book of Records* she is listed as the world's top-selling author.

In 1978 she sang an *Album of Love Songs* with the Royal Philharmonic Orchestra.

940735

In private life Barbara Cartland, who is a Dame of Grace of the Order of St. John of Jerusalem, Chairman of the St. John Council in Hertfordshire and Deputy President of the St. John Ambulance Brigade, has fought for better conditions and salaries for midwives and nurses.

She championed the cause for the elderly in 1956 invoking a Government Enquiry into the "Housing Conditions of Old People."

In 1962 as a result of her work, the law of England was changed so that local authorities had to provide camps for their own gypsies. This has meant that since then thousands and thousands of gypsy children have been able to go to school which they had never been able to do in the past, as their caravans were moved every twenty-four hours by the police.

There are now fourteen camps in Hertfordshire and Barbara Cartland has her own Romany gypsy camp called Barbaraville by the gypsies.

Her designs, "Decorating with Love," are being sold all over the USA and the National Home Fashions League made her in 1981, "Woman of Achievement."

Barbara Cartland's book *Getting Older, Growing Younger*, has been published in Great Britain and the USA and her fifth cookery book, *The Romance of Food*, is now being used by the House of Commons.

In 1984 she received, at Kennedy Airport, America's Bishop Wright Air Industry Award for her contribution to the development of aviation. In 1931 she and two RAF officers thought of, and carried, the first aeroplane-towed glider air-mail.

During the War she was Chief Lady Welfare Officer in Bedfordshire looking after 20,000 Service men and women. She thought of having a pool of wedding dresses at the War Office so a service bride could hire a gown for the day.

She bought 1,000 secondhand gowns without coupons for the ATS, the WAAF and the WRNS. In 1945 Barbara Cartland received the Certificate of Merit from Eastern Command.

In 1964 Barbara Cartland founded the National Association for Health, of which she is the President, as a front for all the Health Stores and for any product made as alternative medicine.

This has now a £600 million a year turnover, with one third going in export.

In January 1988 she received 'La Médaille de Vermeil de la Ville de Paris" (The Gold Medal of Paris). This is the highest award to be given by the City of Paris for ACHIEVEMENT – 25 million books sold in France.

In March 1988 Barbara Cartland was asked by the Indian Government to open their Health Resort outside Delhi. This is almost the largest Health Resort in the world.

Barbara Cartland was received with great enthusiasm by her fans, who also fêted her at a reception in the city and she received the gift of an embossed plate from the Government.

Barbara Cartland was made a Dame of the Order of

the British Empire in the 1991 New Year's Honours List, by Her Majesty the Queen for her contribution to literature and for her work for the community.

Dame Barbara has now written the greatest number of books by a British author, passing the 564 books written by John Creasey.

AWARDS

1945   Received Certificate of Merit, Eastern Command, for being Welfare Officer to 5,000 troops in Bedfordshire.

1953   Made a Commander of the Order of St. John of Jerusalem. Invested by HRH The Duke of Gloucester at Buckingham Palace.

1972   Invested as Dame of Grace of the Order of St. John in London by The Lord Prior, Lord Caccia.

1981   Received "Achiever of the Year" from the National Home Furnishing Association in Colorado Springs, USA for her designs for wallpaper and fabrics.

1984   Received Bishop Wright Air Industry Award at Kennedy Airport, for inventing the aeroplane-towed Glider.

1988   Received from Monsieur Chirac, the Prime Minister, The Gold Medal of the City of Paris, at the Hôtel de la Ville, Paris, for selling 25 million books and giving a lot of employment.

1991   Invested as Dame of the Order of The British Empire, by HM The Queen at Buckingham Palace for her contribution to literature.

OTHER BOOKS BY
BARBARA CARTLAND

Romantic novels, over 500, the most recently published being:

Love and War	A Coronation of Love
Love at the Ritz	A Duel of Jewels
The Dangerous Marriage	The Duke is Trapped
Good or Bad	Just a Wonderful Dream
This is Love	Love and a Cheetah
Seek the Stars	Drena and The Duke
Running Away to Love	A Dog, A Horse and A Heart
Look with the Heart	Never Lose Love
Safe in Paradise	Spirit of Love
Love in the Ruins	The Eyes of Love

The Dream and the Glory (In aid of the St. John Ambulance Brigade)

Autobiographical and Biographical:

The Isthmus Years 1919–1939
The Years of Opportunity 1939–1945
I Search for Rainbows 1945–1976
We Danced All Night 1919–1929
Ronald Cartland (With a foreword by Sir Winston Churchill)
Polly – My Wonderful Mother
I Seek the Miraculous

Historical:

Bewitching Women
The Outrageous Queen (The Story of Queen Christina
  of Sweden)
The Scandalous Life of King Carol
The Private Life of Charles II
The Private Life of Elizabeth, Empress of Austria
Josephine, Empress of France
Diane de Poitiers
Metternich – The Passionate Diplomat
A Year of Royal Days
Royal Jewels
Royal Eccentrics
Royal Lovers

Sociology:

You in the Home
The Fascinating Forties
Marriage for Moderns
Be Vivid, Be Vital
Love, Life and Sex
Vitamins for Vitality
Husbands and Wives
Men are Wonderful

Etiquette
The Many Facets of Love
Sex and the Teenager
The Book of Charm
Living Together
The Youth Secret
The Magic of Honey
The Book of Beauty and
  Health

Keep Young and Beautiful by Barbara Cartland and
  Elinor Glyn
Etiquette for Love and Romance
Barbara Cartland's Book of Health

Cookery:

Barbara Cartland's Health Food Cookery Book
Food for Love
Magic of Honey Cookbook
Recipes for Lovers
The Romance of Food

Editor of:

The Common Problem by Ronald Cartland (with a preface by the Rt. Hon. the Earl of Selborne, PC)
Barbara Cartland's Library of Love
Library of Ancient Wisdom
Written with Love. Passionate love letters selected by Barbara Cartland

Drama:

Blood Money
French Dressing

Philosophy:

Touch the Stars

Radio Operetta:

The Rose and the Violet (Music by Mark Lubbock) Performed in 1942.

Radio Plays:

The Caged Bird: An episode in the life of Elizabeth Empress of Austria. Performed in 1957.

General:

Barbara Cartland's Book of Useless Information with
    a Foreword by the Earl Mountbatten of Burma.
    (In aid of the United World Colleges)
Love and Lovers (Picture Book)
The Light of Love (Prayer Book)
Barbara Cartland's Scrapbook
    (In aid of the Royal Photographic Museum)
Romantic Royal Marriages
Barbara Cartland's Book of Celebrities
Getting Older, Growing Younger

Verse:

Lines on Life and Love

Music:

An Album of Love Songs sung with the Royal Philharmonic Orchestra.

Films:

A Hazard of Hearts
The Lady and the Highwayman
A Ghost in Monte Carlo

Cartoons:

Barbara Cartland Romances (Book of Cartoons) has
    recently been published in the USA, Great Britain,
    and other parts of the world.

Children:

A Children's Pop-Up Book: Princess to the Rescue

Videos:

A Hazard of Hearts
The Lady and The Highwayman
A Ghost in Monte Carlo

AUTHOR'S NOTE

When I was in Milan in connection with the film that was being made about my novel *A Ghost in Monte Carlo*, I visited the beautiful Cathedral, and found my inspiration for this book.

The Duomo is the most magnificent building in Gothic Italy and was begun in 1386. The cruciform interior has a double-aisled nave 157 ft. high and a pentagonal apse with 52 tall columns.

The builders believed that the higher they could make the Cathedral, the nearer they were to God.

From the topmost gallery there is a magnificent view of the city, the Lombardy Plain, the Alps of Monte Viso and the Apennines.

Chapter One

1882

Luella walked into the Cathedral and sat down at the end of a pew near one of the side-chapels. The light was dim inside the great building except for a multitude of candles burning in the different chapels. She felt the peace of it like a soft hand touching her forehead. The misery she had been feeling all day abated a little.

She had come straight from the cemetery in which her father's funeral had taken place. She had not wanted to return to the small hotel where she had been staying with her father only a short distance from the Cathedral. Ever since they had arrived in Milan she had come to the Cathedral day after day with her father. He had been writing another book, this time on the cathedrals and churches of Europe.

Richard Hanley had already made a name for himself with his book on the temples of Greece. He had decided that the next should be about churches. "There is so much history in them, my dear," he had replied when Luella had questioned him. "They are a landmark in every country which illustrates its development through the ages."

It was the sort of remark her father always made, which left Luella thinking about it afterwards. Invariably, she realised, he had spoken perceptively.

Now he had left her and she was completely alone. She thought that only in the Cathedral could she work out quietly and without panic what to do next.

When her mother died of a fever a year before, she had thought her world had come to an end. But her father had turned to her for support and comfort, and she had known that she must dedicate her life to looking after him. Without her mother he was like a ship without a rudder. She understood then, even more acutely than she had before, how indivisible they each were from the other. Neither of them could live without the other.

In this last year she had watched her father grow weaker and weaker. She had been aware, without putting it into words, that he was slipping away from her. When he caught a cold through his insistence on going up to the roof of the Cathedral one chilly night, it had gone to his chest. It was then she realised that he was making no effort to recover. He was, in fact, counting the hours until he could be with his wife again.

In desperation Luella had sent for the most experienced doctors in Milan. They could do nothing but prescribe expensive medicines which her father refused to take saying they would do him no good. Now when she wanted to weep because he had left her she knew she was crying for herself. Her father had no wish to live when his wife was no longer there beside him. "They are happy now," Luella thought, "but what about . . me?"

It was certainly a problem. She had paid for her father's funeral knowing she was spending all the money they had left. There was no more money in her father's account in the Italian bank and Luella doubted if there was anything left in England.

Because she had travelled with her parents ever since she had been born, she was practical, and she knew what she had to do. Her father had told her often enough that the British Embassies were there to help any British in trouble abroad. Luella was certain that the Embassy would provide her with her fare back to England.

Thinking about it, she realised she did not know, once she got there, where she could go. Her mother had run away to get married to her father. Her grandparents had been furious and had vowed they would never speak to her mother again. And as far as Luella knew, her father's family were scattered in different parts of England. Because he was continually travelling he seldom heard from them. She was not even certain whether or not his brother was still alive.

She regretted now that she had been so remiss in not finding out more about her relatives or at least learning their names. But, because she was always moving with her parents from one country to another,

England seemed very far away. Luella had visited it only twice in the whole of her life.

The first time she was very small and they went to Cornwall. She could remember an attractive house where her father had been born. He had returned home because his mother was seriously ill and they had stayed for nearly a month until to everybody's surprise the invalid recovered. She did not, in fact, die for another six years.

The second time Luella visited England was when her father went to receive the award of 'Book of the Year'. It was for the one he had written about Greece. Neither her father nor her mother wanted to keep in touch with their relations. They were in London for only a week and left immediately after the presentation had taken place.

After her father had been acclaimed, Luella had asked: "How does it feel to be famous, Papa?"

"It amused me to see my fellow authors grinding their teeth," her father replied, "but otherwise I am quite happy to remain in obscurity." That was the truth. Her father had never sought fame. Luella thought now that had he done so, her present predicament might not have been so serious.

"What shall I do? What shall I do?" she asked and she started to pray. Her mother had always told her that every prayer, however small, was heard. Luella prayed even while she thought it unlikely she could be helped. She did not want to travel to England alone, nor to try to find her relatives, whose names she did not even know. She prayed for a long time.

At last, sitting back in an ancient carved pew, she

became aware that in the chapel on her left-hand side a wedding ceremony was taking place. The Cathedral was so large that she had not been aware of the bride and bridegroom passing up the aisle. Now she could see them standing before the priest. The altar behind him was decorated with flowers and six lighted candles. The bride, Luella thought, looked very attractive. She and her bridegroom both seemed very young.

There were no witnesses. Luella wondered if they were, in fact, making a run-away marriage as her mother and father had done. The ceremony took a long time because they received the Eucharist. Luella sat watching, and thought the young couple were very much in love. They behaved as if this was the most exciting and romantic moment of their lives.

There were two servers attending the priest. They wore short white surplices edged with beautifully made antique lace. They seemed to blend in with the flowers, the candles and the scent of incense. It all made for Luella a picture of beauty and she watched the wedding until it ended.

After the blessing the bride and bridegroom went to the side of the chapel to sign the register. The bride threw back her veil. Having signed the book she returned to the centre of the chapel and Luella could see her face clearly. Italian, with dark hair and large sparkling dark eyes, she was very pretty. Her bridegroom was also Italian, taller than usual and handsome.

"I hope they will be happy," Luella thought. She wondered what difficulties and problems lay ahead of them. There would certainly be some, otherwise their parents would have been present at the ceremony.

The priest walked with them to the entrance of the chapel and they thanked him before they moved down the aisle. Luella watched them as they walked towards the West Door; she noticed that the priest went in the opposite direction. Meanwhile his two servers had picked up the chalice containing the Eucharist to take it back to the sanctuary. The candles were still burning on the altar.

Now Luella saw another priest, wearing a black cassock, hurrying into the chapel where the couple had just been married. He looked to right and left of him, then went to the altar steps. Watching him, Luella thought he was about to kneel and say a prayer. Instead, without even genuflecting, he walked to the side where the bride and bridegroom had signed the register. He appeared to be very interested in the book and studied it for two or three minutes.

Then the two servers came back. As they entered the chapel the priest turned quickly and walked out past them, almost pushing them out of his way as he did so. They looked at each other in surprise and stared after him. He hurried away down the aisle which led to the West Door. The servers exchanged a few words and shrugged their shoulders. Going to the altar they blew out the candles. One of them picked up the register and they moved back down the aisle from where they had just returned.

Intrigued by what was happening, Luella had for the moment forgotten her own problems. Now with a little sigh she knew she must go to the British Embassy and tell them her tale of woe. It was an uncomfortable and unpleasant thing to have to do. But the money she had in her handbag was not enough, she knew, even to pay the bill at the hotel. She could not even be sure that there was enough to pay for a meal this evening. She could only hope that the consul or whoever she saw in the Embassy would have heard of her father. If so, she hoped he would be impressed by his fame as an author, at least sufficiently to make him kinder towards her than he might otherwise be.

Luella was sure that the Embassy was continually plagued by English people who went abroad, then ran out of money. They would be unlikely to provide her with a chaperon, which was something her mother would have insisted on. Luella wanted to believe she could look after herself. But she knew travelling alone would be very much more difficult than when she had her parents with her.

Now that she was eighteen she was extremely pretty. She would have been very stupid if she had not known that with her fair hair and blue eyes she attracted attention from the dark Italian men. Wherever she went they always made excuses to get into conversation with her. It was only because her father was a ferocious watchdog where his daughter was concerned that they were not able to make a nuisance of themselves.

"I will manage, I *have* to manage!" Luella told herself. Nevertheless, she was apprehensive.

She walked down the aisle and out by the West Door. After the gloom inside the huge building, the sunshine seemed to blind her eyes. Because the

Cathedral had meant so much to her father, she turned to look back at it.

"The Duomo," he had said, "is the most magnificent Gothic building in northern Italy." It was certainly spectacular, Luella thought, with its high dome and four towers. The *façade*, which her father had told her was not completed until 1813, was different from and certainly more impressive than that of any other cathedral she had seen.

She tipped back her head to look up at it. It was then a voice beside her said: "I see you are admiring our beautiful Cathedral, Signorina. As I expect you know, those who built it so high believed that the higher they went, the nearer they got to God."

Luella had started when the man had first spoken to her and thought quickly she should move away. As he finished speaking she turned to look at him. He was, she saw, a middle-aged man with greying hair under his hat, and smartly dressed. Before she could reply he said: "I feel sure you are English, and we always consider it a compliment if the English admire our churches and buildings when they have so many beautiful examples in their own country."

"The Cathedral certainly is very fine!" Luella agreed.

She knew she should move away and had already started to walk the first few steps when the stranger said: "Forgive me if I sound impertinent, Signorina, but, surely you are not alone?"

Because he sounded so shocked by the idea, Luella answered: "I . . I am afraid I am, but my hotel is just around the corner."

"Then perhaps you will allow me to escort you there," the stranger said. "Anyone as beautiful as you is bound to attract attention from impudent and undesirable young men who have nothing better to do."

He spoke English very fluently, despite an Italian accent, and Luella gave a little laugh. "If I walk quickly," she said, "I doubt if anybody will attempt to accost me."

"Nevertheless, Signorina, I feel it my duty to see you are safe," the stranger persisted.

Looking round, Luella was aware that he had some reason for what he was saying. There were several young Italians sitting on the steps up to the Cathedral, watching her as if she was some form of entertainment.

"I am, in fact," she said, "going now to the British Embassy, which I believe is not far from here."

"Then you are going back to England?" the stranger enquired.

"It is . . something I have to do," Luella said. "You see . . my father . . has . . d.died." She could not help her voice breaking on the last words.

The man beside her gave a little murmur of sympathy. "So you are all alone," he remarked. "A terrible predicament for a beautiful young Englishwoman in a strange country."

"I . . I shall be . . all right," Luella said, "and thank you for being so consolatory."

She would have walked away, but he moved beside her. "As you so rightly said, your Embassy is only two streets away," he said, "but it seems a pity that you must go home when Italy is so beautiful in the spring."

Luella smiled. "It was Robert Browning who said: 'Oh, to be in England, now that April's there.' " It was the sort of remark she would have made to her father.

Somehow the man beside her, who was obviously over forty, seemed like a fatherly figure. "It is a pity that you cannot see more of Italy," he said reflectively.

As he walked along beside her Luella noticed another small group of young men staring at her, and she could not help feeling glad that she was not alone. "I have already seen quite a lot of your country," she replied. "My parents came often to Rome and his account of this beautiful Cathedral was to complete my father's new book, if he had been able to . . finish it."

"Your father was a writer?" the man beside her asked.

"His name was Richard Hanley," Luella replied. "His book on Greek temples was published in Italy, as well as in other countries."

"Then of course I have heard his name!" the stranger exclaimed. They walked on a little way before he said: "If you are going to the Embassy, Signorina, and I have guessed that you need them to help you to return to England, could you not stay a little longer? I would like to show you the Royal Palace, which is very beautiful."

"That is very kind of you," Luella said, "but I cannot afford to stay here any longer."

The man beside her stopped. "You have no money!" he exclaimed. "Surely that is impossible!"

"I think perhaps there will be some in England," Luella replied, "but my father's funeral took up all we had left in Italy."

The stranger nodded his head. "I can understand that. Funerals are always expensive wherever they take place. But, instead of your leaving so hurriedly, Signorina, I have a suggestion to make."

Because he had stopped and was standing still, Luella felt it would be rude to walk on. She was therefore obliged to stand with him. She looked up at him enquiringly and he said: "I wonder if you would consider a little employment in Milan which would be easy for you to carry out and is very highly paid."

Luella hesitated and he said: "I will not try to persuade you if you are anxious to return immediately to England, but it does seem to me that I could offer you an opportunity for enjoying herself, and also of making a considerable amount of money."

"What would I have to do?" Luella enquired.

As she spoke a carriage went by and the stranger could not answer her until the noise of the wheels and the clatter of the hoofs had faded into the distance. "It is difficult to talk here," he said. "Will you honour me by coming to my office which is not far away? Then I can explain to you very simply what would be required."

Luella started to say, "I think I had best go to the British Embassy," when another carriage passed. Behind it came a carriage that was for hire. The man beside her raised his hand and the coachman reined in his horse. It was an open carriage and without saying any more the stranger helped Luella into it.

She thought as he did so that perhaps she was making a mistake. She was talking and listening to a strange man to whom she had not been introduced. At the same time she felt there was no reason why she should not at least hear his suggestion, although it might be difficult to stay on in Italy, however attractive his proposition.

Then she remembered the uncertainty of what she might find in England. She told herself that it could do no harm to hear what this gentleman, for he was undoubtedly that, had to say. After all, if she was not interested, she could still go to the British Embassy.

The gentleman gave the address to the coachman and, as he drove off, he said: "Now this is more comfortable than walking, and suppose we introduce ourselves? My name is Vittorio Vecchio."

"You already know, Signor, that my name is Hanley," Luella said, "and I was given the Italian Christian name of Luella because I was born in Italy."

"A very charming name for a very charming lady," Signor Vecchio said, "and I am sure, Miss Hanley, that your distinguished father would advise you to listen to what I have to suggest."

Luella thought it was kind of the Signor to talk of her father in such a way.

They drove on in silence. As the Signor had said, not far from the Cathedral there was an impressive-looking house. The carriage pulled up and Signor Vecchio paid the cabman. They walked up to the house, but to Luella's surprise he did not knock on the front door. Instead he led her down a narrow passageway at the side of the house.

He stopped at another door which he opened with a latch-key. "I am taking you to my office," he said, "because there we shall be undisturbed and it is easier to talk business."

He smiled as he spoke as if he thought 'business' was a strange word to connect with Luella.

His office consisted of a small room with a desk. At the same time there were several comfortable armchairs. On one wall was a large mirror. On another were some paintings which reminded Luella of those she had seen in Paris painted by those who were known as the 'Impressionists'.

Signor Vecchio indicated a chair which had its back to them. "Now what I am sure you would like, and what I would like myself, is a cup of coffee – unless of course, you prefer a different sort of drink?"

Quite suddenly, for no apparent reason, Luella became frightened. She wondered why she had been stupid enough to come here with this stranger. She wanted to leave immediately, but she was not certain how she could do so. It was not just the atmosphere of the room. It was the smile on Signor Vecchio's face. It made him appear different from the fatherly figure who had spoken to her outside the Cathedral. Perhaps it was because he had taken off his hat. Whatever it was, he no longer seemed like the kindly elderly gentleman he had appeared to be on their way here.

"No, no," she said quickly. "It is very kind of you, but I want nothing. Tell me what you have to say, then I will be on my way to the Embassy."

"I am hoping that what I have to say will convince you that you need not go to the Embassy," Signor Vecchio replied. "But of course, my dear young lady, it is entirely up to you." He made a gesture with his hands which was very explicit. At the same time, Luella was sure she should go at once and not listen to him.

"I am going to give the order for the coffee," he said, "and if you do not need it, then of course, you may leave it. It is black, delicious, and very sweet, as you are yourself."

Luella was again frightened. She did not know exactly why she was frightened, but she was. Then as Signor Vecchio moved towards the door it opened with a bang.

"*Trovato – Trovato!*" a voice cried speaking Italian, and a man came into the room. He was wearing a black cassock. When Luella looked at him, she realised he was the priest she had seen in the chapel after the wedding – the priest who had hurried away when the servers had appeared, pushing them out of his way as he went. As he came into the room she thought he looked a rather rough man. He did not give an impression of holiness she would have expected of a priest.

"*Guarda! No siamo solo!*" Signor Vecchio said sharply.

The priest stopped in his tracks. "My apologies," he muttered. "I thought you would be alone."

Signor Vecchio turned to Luella. "Will you excuse

me, Signorina, but I must have a word with Father Sebastian. He will not keep me long, but I have something to show him in another room." Without waiting for Luella to reply, he pushed the priest out of the door. Looking back he said over his shoulder: "I shall not be more than two or three minutes." Then he was gone.

Luella glanced at the closed door. It seemed odd that the priest she had watched in the chapel should be here. However it somehow reassured her that she need not be afraid of Signor Vecchio.

She could quite understand why for the moment she had wanted to run away. It was because she had talked to a stranger. That was something her mother and father had never permitted. And yet, if the priest was here, then surely nothing could be wrong.

But he had burst into the room! She wondered why he was so excited at what he said he had found.

Because she was alone, she could now look round the room without appearing inquisitive. She looked at the pictures more closely and there was no doubt they were strange. All of them were of women who had been painted in what were certainly unusual postures.

Then she told herself that she was not at this moment interested in pictures, but in what Signor Vecchio had to offer her. If she did not agree she could be on her way to the British Embassy.

She began to feel sure that any employment the Signor suggested would be something of which neither her father nor her mother would approve. She wondered if because she was young and pretty he might want her to be a saleswoman in a shop. But he did not look like a shop-keeper. She could not imagine what else it could be, unless of course it was something connected with buildings like the Cathedral.

Perhaps he thought she could be a guide. The idea sprang to her mind. Then she was quite sure she was too young and, if she was honest, too pretty to be a guide for men who would undoubtedly pay her too many compliments. "It was a waste of time my coming here," she told herself.

At that moment the door opened and Signor Vecchio came back. He was looking rather serious, and it struck her that perhaps Father Sebastian had done something to annoy him. At the same time it could, of course, be for some other reason.

Signor Vecchio sat down at his desk. "I apologise most profusely," he said, "for the interruption, but now I can put in front of you a very important and interesting proposition to which I hope you will agree."

Chapter Two

Luella turned her face towards Signor Vecchio, thinking as she did so that she was really wasting her
time.

"What I have to tell you is a sad story," Signor
Vecchio began. "Seven years ago I was friendly with
a very beautiful girl called Tia Broletto, and when I
say beautiful, she was strikingly so."

He paused for a moment, then went on: "She fell in
love with a charming and delightful Englishman who
was in the British Army. His name was Ivor Stone and
they were married."

He paused again before continuing: "I thought they
were extremely happy, but one can never judge love
where it concerns other people, and unfortunately
they quarrelled."

Luella was listening, but she could not see how this
could possibly concern her.

"The Captain," Signor Vecchio said, "went back to

his regiment in England, and as far as I know, they never saw each other again."

Luella was wondering how quickly she could get away and go to the British Embassy.

"After he left," Signor Vecchio went on, "Tia gave birth to a son and I imagine she told the Captain that he was now a father."

"But he did not return to see her?" Luella asked, feeling that some comment was expected of her.

"Not that I am aware of," Signor Vecchio replied. "But Tia continued to be one of the most delightful and charming women in Milan." Signor Vecchio's voice deepened as he said: "A week ago Tia died of cancer, and many people were broken-hearted by her death. I assure you, Signorina Hanley, there was not a dry eye at her funeral."

Again there was a pause and Luella murmured: "How . . sad!"

"Very sad indeed," Signor Vecchio said, "especially for her son, Enrico, who is now six years old and should be looked after by his father."

Luella looked surprised. "But surely he has Italian relations?"

"He has indeed," Signor Vecchio agreed, "but in the meantime Enrico's father has become the Duke of Ingatestone."

Luella had heard of the Duke. An English newspaper had been sent to her father because it mentioned his book. In an article suggesting books for Christmas presents, Richard Hanley's book, *The Temples of Greece*, had been recommended. It said that in the opinion of the critic there had never been a better book on the subject.

Because she enjoyed reading the English news-papers, Luella had read the rest of that edition carefully. One of the headlines had claimed that the worst accident of all time had been suffered by the noble and ancient family of Ingatestone.

Apparently the Duke of Ingatestone, who was an elderly man, had travelled to Ireland with his three sons and their children to celebrate the eightieth birthday of the Earl of Kilkelly to whom they were related. There had been a huge party to honour the Earl's birthday, and relatives had come from all over the world. The Kilkellys were descended from the Irish Kings. The Earl had been fêted and congratulated with dinners, a ball and fireworks at the ancestral castle.

On the way back to England disaster had struck. There was thick fog and the ship in which the Duke of Ingatestone and his family were travelling collided with a fully laden cargo-boat. Both ships sank with nearly all lives lost.

It was such a dramatic story that Luella had read it, thinking how dangerous the sea could be. She had remembered times when travelling with her father they had encountered sudden storms. They had been bad enough to make her feel that the ship would capsize at any moment.

Luella remembered reading that the Dukedom of Ingatestone had passed to the son of the Duke's younger brother. He had not accompanied them to Ireland because he had been on duty at Windsor Castle.

Watching the expression on her face, Signor Vecchio

said: "I see you have heard of the present Duke."

"I read of the tragedy that occurred to his family when they were drowned at sea," Luella replied.

"It was in our newspapers too," Signor Vecchio remarked. "Naturally I was interested because young Captain Stone, now the Duke, had succeeded to such an important position." He hesitated as if he was feeling for words before he said: "I tried to persuade Tia to join her husband,but she refused."

"They had not been divorced?" Luella enquired.

"Signor Vecchio threw out his hands. "Who can obtain a divorce in England when it has to go before Parliament?" he asked. "And Tia was a Catholic. As far as she was concerned, she had made a vow to be married to one man and one man only." He spoke dramatically.

Luella felt embarrassed that she had asked such a question.

Then almost as if he was speaking to himself, Signor Vecchio went on: "Now that Tia is dead, her son's proper place is with his father. He must be brought up to inherit the position which will be his by right."

Now Luella could understand the point of the story.

However, before she could say anything, Signor Vecchio added: "I want you to take Enrico to England and make sure his father welcomes him and accepts him as his son and heir."

There was silence.

Then Luella said hesitatingly: "Surely .. it is .. strange that the Duke has not .. seen his child since he .. was born. It would seem that he is .. not very interested in him."

"I am afraid once the two young people were no longer in love with each other, they began to lead separate lives," Signor Vecchio explained in a lofty tone. "But now that Tia is dead, I am quite sure the Duke will realise where his duty lies."

"And . . you want . . me to take the . . little boy to . . England?" Luella asked.

"I would be extremely grateful if you will do so," Signor Vecchio replied. "I would have taken him myself, but I am so extremely busy here in Milan that it is impossible for me to get away." He paused for a moment and then continued: "I also feel it would be best for him to be taken by somebody who is English rather than Italian."

"Would he not be . . happier with . . someone he . . knows?" Luella ventured.

"He is a charming child – charming!" Signor Vecchio assured her, "as I am sure you will find when you meet him. And as you are anxious to go back to England, what could be a better arrangement?" He thought for a moment, then he said: "Naturally, as you will be undertaking such an important mission, I will send a courier with you."

Luella drew in her breath. She had been trying to think how she could refuse the Signor's suggestion. Now, almost as if in answer to her prayer, she was to be looked after on the journey. She could not be nervous with a courier to escort her.

As if the Signor was following her thoughts, he said: "I know of an elderly courier who has travelled to England on a number of occasions. He will look after you and little Enrico and see there are no difficulties or problems. Only when you have handed the child over to his father will he return to Italy."

"That would .. certainly be very helpful," Luella said, "but I must explain, Signor, that I was going to the British Embassy to ask for help financially for my journey to England. Having paid for my father's funeral I have no more money in this country."

"Your expenses need not trouble you at all," the Signor said. "Everything will be provided for you, and naturally, I will pay you an appropriate fee for your undertaking such a difficult task in caring for a small child."

Luella's first instinct was to refuse. Then she thought she would be very silly if she did so, she would need money when she arrived in England. She was hoping there would be some money in her father's bank account, or perhaps the publisher of *The Temples of Greece* owed him some royalties. But that was something of which she could not be certain.

At the same time she wished she need not be dependent on Signor Vecchio. She could not explain to herself why. She just knew she did not wish to be beholden to him. Despite the fact that he was doing her a favour, she did not like him.

"Now that is settled," the Signor said briskly. "What I suggest, Signorina, is that I escort you back to your hotel. You can pack your luggage and I will arrange for you to be on the express train for Paris which leaves this evening."

Again Luella wished she could refuse his offer, and tell him that she was not interested. Then she thought she should be thankful not to have to humiliate herself at the British Embassy. And it was specially attractive that he had promised her a courier to escort her back to England. With an effort she answered: "Thank you .. thank you .. very much."

"I will take you back to your hotel," the Signor said. He walked towards the door as he spoke, and there was nothing Luella could do but follow him. She could not explain her reluctance to accept what seemed to be a very generous proposition.

Just before they drove off, Luella looked back at the house and saw Father Sebastian standing at a window watching them. Once again she was conscious that he had a coarse and somewhat unpleasant face. She wondered what he had found that had excited him so much when he had burst into Signor Vecchio's office.

When they reached the hotel Signor Vecchio sent her upstairs to pack and she heard him asking for the proprietor. Luella knew he was settling her bill. Again for no good reason she could think of she found herself resenting the fact that the Signor had taken everything into his own hands.

"I should be grateful, very grateful, that this opportunity has occurred," she told herself, "and it must have come in answer to my prayers to Mama and Papa. At the same time I cannot help feeling there is something wrong .. although I do not know what it is."

It did not take her long to pack her own clothes and the few things belonging to her father that she wanted to keep. There were a number of books already in a case. She had only to include one or two more before she closed the lid and locked it.

There was no point in taking her father's clothes with her. She therefore asked the chambermaid to accept them and get what she could for them. The maid burst into a flood of Italian as she expressed her gratitude. It was this that made Luella remember that Signor Vecchio was not aware that she spoke Italian. He had very carefully spoken to her all the time they had been together in English. Again for no reason she could think of, it seemed wrong that she wished to keep the fact of her knowledge of Italian a secret from him.

Her luggage was ready to be carried downstairs. She suddenly thought that the little boy, Enrico, would only be able to speak Italian. She went down the stairs followed by a maid carrying her bags.

Signor Vecchio was there waiting for her, and she said: "I have been thinking, Signor, that the little boy will . . speak only . . Italian."

"That is where you are wrong," Signor Vecchio replied. "Enrico has been taking English lessons for two months." He saw the look of surprise on Luella's face and said: "I arranged it because as soon as I knew that Tia could not recover and would die, I decided that her son must go to his father."

"So he has been learning to speak English," Luella murmured.

"You must speak English all the way on the journey," Signor Vecchio said in a commanding tone. "It is very important that his father should not think of him as Italian, when he is half English and has an English title."

"I will do that," Luella agreed.

"Enrico is the Marquess of Gates, and the family name is Stone," the Signor added.

While they were talking Luella's luggage was being put on the carriage. The Signor took her down the passageway and helped her inside. He then got in himself and as they drove off she asked him: "Where was the Duke married? Was it in the Cathedral?"

"Yes, of course," the Signor replied. "It was a quiet wedding, but it gave me great pleasure to see two people so much in love with each other."

Luella thought they might have been like the young bride and bridegroom she had watched earlier in the day being married. Then she remembered that when speaking of divorce the Signor had said that Tia was a Catholic, so presumably the Duke was not a Catholic and it would have been a very short service.

It only took a short time for them to reach another street in which there were some poor-looking houses. The carriage stopped outside one and the Signor said: "There is no need for you to get out. I will collect Enrico and take you both to an hotel near the station, where you can rest until the train is due."

Luella did not say anything and he quickly climbed out of the carriage. She had the feeling that he had no wish for her to go into the dingy-looking house. It seemed to her strange. If the child's mother, Tia, had been such a social success as the Signor implied, why should she have lived with her son in such a sordid neighbourhood?

The Signor was not as long as she expected. He came out quite soon holding the hand of a small boy. When Luella saw him she thought he was attractive.

At the same time he looked completely Italian. He jumped into the carriage, obviously excited at being taken for a ride.

He had dark hair and his eyes were large, dark and very expressive. He also, unexpectedly, had two peculiarities. One was that his hair grew on his forehead into a 'widow's peak', which one usually saw only on women. Secondly, his dark eyebrows turned up at the ends, which gave him the look of a small gnome or goblin. It was an unusual distinction but rather attractive.

"Here is Enrico," the Signor said, "and he has been told he is to travel to England with a very charming lady."

Enrico held out his hand. "I . . wanta to go . . een beeg . . sheep," he said slowly, speaking in English.

"But first we have to go in a train for a long time," Luella said.

The small boy smiled. " 'Rico like beeg – train," he said. "Go verry . . verry.fast!"

"That is good, Enrico!" Signor Vecchio said. "You speak very good English."

" 'Rico verry clever," the boy answered. "I spik lot an' lot of Engleesh. N.no m.morre Italian." He stumbled a little over the words, but not very badly.

Luella thought he must have worked extremely hard to have learnt so much English so quickly. She was to find however as they drove on that he spoke rapid Italian whenever he saw something that interested him. They saw some dogs fighting which excited him and he forgot his English when there was a balloon floating overhead. Luella carefully talked to him in

English in front of the Signor. The boy seemed to understand more or less everything she said.

The hotel near the station was quite a comfortable one and the Signor ordered them tea. "You are English, Signorina," he said, "and therefore you expect to have tea at four o'clock and Enrico must expect the same."

Enrico was only too willing to gobble up the food that the Signor ordered. But he drank orangeade rather than tea.

As they ate, Luella was aware that the Signor's eyes kept darting towards the door as if he was expecting somebody. Finally, after they had been in the hotel for nearly an hour a man appeared, and he jumped hastily to his feet. They talked for a moment in the doorway, then the Signor took the newcomer to a far corner of the room, where they were out of hearing of both Luella and Enrico. They remained there for some time. Glancing in their direction, Luella was aware that he was giving the man who had just arrived some money. There appeared to be quite a lot of it.

When finally the man left, the Signor came back to the tea-table. He sat down beside Luella and said in a grave voice: "Now what I have here for you, Signorina, is of very great importance. It is a letter to the Duke telling him of Tia's death and explaining why I have sent Enrico in your charge to England."

"Do you mean you have not yet notified the Duke that you are sending him his son?"

"There has been no time," the Signor replied. "It was something I intended to do as soon as Tia died, but I was desperate as to whom I could entrust Enrico.

I wanted him to reach England in the charge of an English person, not an Italian."

He saw that Luella was looking uncomfortable and he went on quickly: "I assure you that the Duke will welcome his son. It is just that there has not been enough time since Tia's funeral for me to find someone like yourself to take Enrico to England." He smiled and putting out his hand laid it on Luella's. "I am very, very grateful," he said, "in fact I think as I waited outside the Cathedral you must have come to me in answer to my prayer."

He stopped speaking for a moment and then went on: "Who could be more suitable to take the Marquess to his father the Duke, than the daughter of so distinguished a writer?"

There was nothing Luella could say, at the same time she felt extremely uncomfortable. When she found her voice, she said: "I think what you must do, Signor, is to write immediately to the Duke and tell him that Enrico is on his way or, better still, send a telegram."

The Signor made a very Italian gesture. "Telegrams, my dear young lady, are too often a disaster. They never appear to arrive at their destination, however carefully they are inscribed."

"Then, please, you will write?" Luella persisted.

"But of course I will do that, as soon as you have left," the Signor promised. "But it will not arrive before you reach England. You can, however, alert the Duke that it is on its way."

"Then promise me you will not forget," Luella begged.

"How could I forget anything, dear lady, you ask of me?" he replied in honeyed tones.

Luella was suspicious all the same that he would not keep his promise. It was too late now to suggest they should stay longer in Italy and wait until the Duke was aware that they were on their way. She took the letter which the Signor had handed her. It was addressed to the Duke, and she put it into her handbag.

As if he had no wish to talk about it further, the Signor then gave her some money for the journey. "This is just to buy anything you need for yourself," he explained. "The courier will settle all the tips as well as seeing to your tickets."

"You are . . very kind," Luella murmured.

As she spoke the door of the room where they were having tea opened again. The Signor sprang to his feet. This time it was a middle-aged man with whitening hair who looked, Luella thought, as if he might be the courier.

The Signor hurried towards him, and again took him into a corner where he talked to him earnestly. Again there was an exchange of money, and finally the Signor came back to the table bringing the courier with him. "This, Signorina," he said, "is Alberto Drago."

Luella shook him by the hand and he replied in good English that it was a privilege to escort her to England. The Signor then looked at a gold watch he took from his waistcoat pocket. "It is time," he said, "for us to go to the station." The luggage was collected by a porter and the courier went ahead to purchase the tickets.

There was a long wait before the train arrived at the station. Luella knew that Signor Vecchio was impatient for them to be on their way. He did not talk very much, but kept looking down the line, waiting for the train to appear. When finally it drew up to the platform he hurried them into a carriage.

As soon as they were seated and the courier joined them he said goodbye. "I am exceedingly grateful to you, Signorina," he said. "You are doing a kind action which I am sure you will never regret."

He said goodbye to Enrico and nodded to the courier. "Contact me," he said sharply, "as soon as you return."

"*Si, Signor,*" Alberto Drago replied.

The Signor then walked away and was quickly lost in the crowd milling about on the platform. Luella gave a little sigh. She could not help feeling that everything had happened too quickly, and it was a mistake to be in such a hurry. She wished she had insisted they should wait until the Duke learnt of their intended arrival. However it was too late now. She could only feel she had been swept on a tidal wave into strange waters that might prove to be dangerous.

" 'Rico go Eengland een a beeg sheep, a verry beeg sheep!" Enrico was saying. He was running up and down the carriage as he spoke, excited at being in the train.

"Come and sit down, Enrico," Luella said, "and I will tell you a story."

"Tella me a story about a beega sheep," Enrico ordered.

"If that is what you want," Luella answered.

At the same time she was thinking that it was a ship

that had sunk which was responsible for her being here. And for Enrico, a little Italian boy, becoming the heir to the Duke of Ingatestone.

She wondered, if his father were still just Captain Ivor Stone, whether Signor Vecchio would have been so anxious to send the child to England to join him. There was also the question in her mind as to whether or not the Duke would be pleased to see Enrico. It made Luella feel once again she was doing the wrong thing.

"It is all rather frightening," she told herself. As she did so she heard the guard blow his whistle.

Then she knew that, for better or worse, she was on her way to England with a courier to look after her and with a small Italian boy whose father did not yet know he was on his way from Italy.

Chapter Three

The new experience of being on a train soon grew boring for Enrico. At first he ran from side to side looking at the countryside through which they were passing. Then it grew dark and he was tired. Luella tucked him up with a rug the courier had brought with him and he was soon sound asleep.

It seemed a long night.

When they stopped in the morning Luella was glad to get out and walk to the restaurant on the station. She longed for a bath to wash away the smell and dust of the train. She knew, however, it would be a long time before she could have one.

Enrico and the courier both ate a good breakfast, but Luella did not feel hungry. She was, however, glad of the hot coffee. Yet for some reason it reminded her of the coffee that Signor Vecchio had offered her. She remembered how in a strange way the offer had made her feel frightened.

Now she decided she had been very foolish to be frightened of the Signor. Yet she knew there was something about him which she disliked although she could not put it into words.

They set off again, Enrico demanding to be told stories that kept him amused for a little while. Then he wandered about the carriage which fortunately they had to themselves. The courier gave him some small coins to play with which he used like tiddleywinks. Altogether it was a very long day, and the next one seemed even longer.

When they arrived in Paris they had to change trains. The wait between enabled Luella to go to the Ladies' cloakroom and wash Enrico's face and hands as well as her own. She had travelled too long with her father not to be able to make herself comfortable even in the most unlikely places.

She had never cared particularly for trains and preferred travelling by ship. When they set off again it was a relief to know that they were at last getting nearer to England. Enrico talked incessantly about the 'beeg sheep' in which they were to travel across the Channel.

It was a pleasant surprise when they got to Calais to find it was a sunny day, the sea was calm, and the ship was not too crowded. Enrico wanted to run round the decks. Alberto Drago shared the responsibility with Luella to ensure that he did not fall overboard. Finally the white cliffs of Dover came in sight. Luella thought she had never been more pleased to see the shores of England.

But there was yet another train journey to London.

Now she began to feel afraid. She knew instinctively that Signor Vecchio had not sent a letter to the Duke as he had promised he would. She was certain that he had every intention of breaking his promise.

However, when they arrived at the station it was still early in the afternoon. The courier hired a hackney carriage and ordered the driver to take them to Gatestone House in Park Lane. London looked exciting, the buildings impressive, the trees and flowers in the park colourful. When they arrived it seemed a large and very impressive mansion.

Now Luella was feeling extremely nervous and her heart was beating uncomfortably in her breast. Alberto Drago got out of the carriage first. He knocked on the front door and spoke to the footman who opened it. The footman then fetched the butler who had a long conversation with Mr Drago.

Luella could not hear what was being said. However, it did not surprise her when the courtier came back to say that the Duke was in the country. If they wanted to contact him they would have to go to Gatestone Castle in Berkshire.

Although it was a setback, Luella could not help giving a little sigh of relief. She had no wish to meet the Duke when she was feeling tired and dishevelled by a long journey. She thought too that Enrico was looking untidy and rather dirty.

"Surely we cannot go there tonight?" she asked the courier.

"No, of course not," he replied. "It is a long distance, and I shall have to hire a carriage, or rather, what is called here a 'post-chaise'."

Luella knew that meant they would change horses at a posting inn. "How long will it take us?" she asked.

"I will have to find out," Alberto Drago replied, "but I think it will take most of the day to get there."

While they were talking the cabman was waiting for instructions. Finally the courier gave him the name of an hotel. "We shall have to stay the night," he said, "and I expect like me, Miss Hanley, you will be glad of a comfortable bed."

"I will indeed!" Luella replied.

The hotel, which was in Paddington, was not particularly impressive. But it was quiet, and the bedroom into which Luella was shown was small, but clean.

Enrico was next door and after he had explored their rooms he was quite ready to lie down and go to sleep. Luella could not help thinking that if he were an English boy he would doubtless have been more obstreperous.

Once he was asleep she went downstairs to ask the proprietor if it was possible to have a bath. It certainly caused a commotion. Finally a chambermaid and the man who had carried in their luggage brought a hip-bath into the bedroom. An hour later they produced two cans of warm water. Luella could wash completely. But there was nothing to dry herself on except a small and worn Turkish towel.

After her bath there was a message from Alberto Drago inviting her to dine with him. She felt he was merely being polite. If she refused his invitation he would feel free to go out and visit some friends. She therefore replied that she would prefer something light in her bedroom.

When the tray was brought up she found there was a thin soup and cold leg of chicken that did not look very appetising. All she really wanted was to sleep and she ate what she could. She then put the tray outside the door and got into bed.

The next thing Luella knew it was morning. Enrico was sitting on the end of her bed playing with a ball that someone had given him. Luella helped the little boy to dress. Then she put on a different gown from the one in which she had travelled yesterday. Having had a good night's sleep, she now felt ready to face the world. Even the Duke did not seem so menacing as he had before.

She took Enrico downstairs for breakfast. They found the courier already there looking drawn and tired. Luella learnt that he had stayed out late with some friends he knew in the neighbourhood.

"I have ordered a carriage," he told her. "I am afraid Signor Vecchio is going to find this trip very expensive."

"I am sure," Luella replied, "the Duke will reimburse him for anything he has expended on Enrico."

She saw an expression of doubt on Alberto Drago's face. It made her think that if the Duke was not pleased to see his son, he might not feel inclined to be generous. "When are we leaving?" she asked a little nervously.

"I could not get a carriage to take us so far until half-past twelve," the courier replied. "We would be wise, therefore, to have something to eat before we leave."

"I think that is sensible," Luella agreed, "but, please, ask the proprietor for something which Enrico will enjoy. As he is not used to English food, he will not have a taste for roast beef and apple pie!"

She was making a joke, and when Alberto Drago realised it he laughed. "The English do eat other things besides that!" he said.

"Have you been here often?" Luella questioned.

"A number of times," he replied, "and I have some friends who are always pleased to see me."

Luella was sure they were the ones who had kept him out so late last night. She was therefore not surprised when they set off on their journey that Alberto Drago fell asleep. He was soon snoring loudly.

Enrico on the other hand was delighted to be on the move again. He begged to be allowed to sit up on the box with the coachman. At the first place they stopped to change horses Luella asked the coachman if he would have Enrico up beside him.

The coachman agreed saying: "If 'e falls orf, Missus, don' blame me! Oi've got a son o' me own, an Oi knows wot mischief they gets up ter!"

Luella told Enrico he had to be very good and not fidget, but just watch the horses. " 'Rico drives them," he pleaded.

"When you are older you can do that," Luella answered, "and perhaps when you are in the country your father will give you a pony."

" 'Rico wanns beeg horse, verry beeg horse!" Enrico said firmly.

"Then you will have to grow very much bigger than you are at the moment," Luella told him.

They set off again, and now it was growing late in the afternoon. Luella asked Alberto Drago how much further they had to go. He did not know, but thought it would not be very much further.

Soon after this they left the main road and were driving along narrow lanes with high hedges. It was now impossible for the two horses to go at all fast. They were also held up for nearly half-an-hour by a farm-wagon in front of them. The lane was far too narrow for them to be able to pass it.

Luella thought it would be a mistake to arrive very late in the evening. Enrico was tired and not at his best. Also she had the feeling that the Duke would, like most men, resent unexpected visitors late in the evening. "Surely we cannot have much further to go?" she asked Mr Drago.

It was then the man who was driving them admitted that he had lost his way. They went on until they came to a public house and their driver went inside to ask for directions. Alberto Drago got out to hold the horses' heads. Luella was sure that, as they, too, were tired, they would not wander away. The coachman did not reappear for a long time. Luella guessed he was not only chatting to the proprietor, but doubtless having a drink while he was doing so. At last he emerged and told them there were another three miles to go.

Luella knew it would take time if the roads were twisted and narrow like those on which they had just been travelling. In fact they were far worse, and they also had to cross two fords. This delighted

Enrico, although Luella was afraid in case the carriage got stuck in the mud and could not go any further.

The sun was sinking when finally they reached a very attractive village. The cottages had thatched roofs and gardens bright with spring flowers. Then there was a high wall obviously enclosing a park and finally two huge magnificent gates. They were surmounted by a coat of arms picked out in gold.

"We have arrived!" Alberto Drago said. "It has been a long journey."

"Far longer than I expected," Luella said.

"I think our coachman took the wrong road," he replied. "If we had come along the main highway, we would have reached here far sooner."

Luella felt it was no use thinking of that now. At least they had reached Gatestone Castle, and that was all that mattered. They went up a drive with huge oak trees on either side of it. Then she saw the Castle high above a lake silhouetted against trees that had obviously been planted as a protection. Looking at it, Luella thought it was like a jewel in a green velvet setting.

Then she remembered that inside would be the Duke! That meant she soon had to face the uncomfortable task of explaining to him why she had come from Italy to bring him his son. She had assumed when they left London that when he accepted Enrico she would return with Alberto Drago. There was no reason why she should be an encumbrance by staying a minute longer than she had to. But now, as it was so late, it could be more difficult. The Duke might feel compelled to offer her some refreshment and a bed for the night.

As they drew nearer to the Castle she said quickly to Alberto Drago: "When I have seen the Duke and handed over Enrico. I would like to go back to London with you." He did not reply, and she thought he looked at her in surprise. She had, however, left it too late to say any more because the carriage was already in the courtyard.

In front of them was a row of stone steps which led up to the front door. The coachman pulled his horses to a standstill. As he had done in London, Alberto Drago got out first and walked up the steps. A footman on duty must have been looking out because before he had reached the top the door was opened. A second later a man who was obviously a butler appeared. When he did so, Alberto Drago came down the steps again and opened the carriage door so that Luella and Enrico could alight.

The little boy ran up the steps, obviously glad to be on the move. Luella, following more slowly, reached the top and said to the butler: "I think you have just been told that we have called to see His Grace."

"His Grace is expecting you, Madam?" the butler asked.

"No, but will you please tell him that we have come from Italy?"

The butler was too well-trained to express his astonishment. He merely said: "If you'll come this way, Madam, I'll inform His Grace that you're here."

The hall into which Luella stepped was certainly

impressive. There was a staircase of carved oak and a large mediaeval fireplace. Also many gold-framed portraits which Luella was sure were of the Ingatestone ancestors. The butler walked ahead. Luella glanced back to see two footmen carrying her trunk up the steps.

Then she realised that behind them the carriage in which they had come and in which now Mr Drago was sitting alone was turning round. She stopped still, and took a step back towards the door. She thought that there must be some mistake. Mr Drago had not realised that she wanted him to wait for her. Then she watched as to her amazement the horses were moving down the drive up which they had come.

She felt her heart sink. She could not imagine why Alberto Drago, who had seemed such a pleasant man, should behave in such a way. Then she knew the answer. Alberto Drago obviously had been given instructions by Signor Vecchio. She was not to be allowed to relinquish her task so lightly.

Because she had stopped, the butler was waiting for her to follow him. When she turned round he went ahead down the corridor. He opened the door of a room and as Luella and Enrico entered, he said: "His Grace is changing for dinner, Madam. I'll inform him of your arrival, but you may have to wait a short time before you can see His Grace."

"Thank you," Luella replied.

As the butler shut the door she saw that they were in a beautifully furnished room. There were pictures on the walls which she knew her mother would have appreciated. There was also a multitude of treasures in cabinets and on tables which she knew would delight her, had she time to look at them.

For the moment, however, she could only worry that Mr Drago had left her in that strange manner. He had been so polite and courteous during the day. It had never struck her for one moment that he would abandon her on Signor Vecchio's instructions in the Duke's Castle.

What was more, she was suddenly aware that he had not, as she had expected he would, given her any money. Signor Vecchio had spoken of her being rewarded for taking Enrico to England. Mr Drago had paid for everything on the journey. Luella had not thought of asking him for the fee that she was to receive for bringing Enrico to England.

Now she was aware with a sinking of her heart that all she possessed were a few Italian coins of low denomination. It was the money Signor Vecchio had handed her before they left Milan. She realised with a sense of horror that she was in a very uncomfortable position. To leave the Castle she would now be obliged to ask the Duke to lend her some money to get back to London.

Enrico was running round the room. He found a snuff-box that was made like a ship and a piece of Dresden china in the form of a bird. Because he was excited he was talking about them in Italian. Luella, too worried to protest, answered him in the same language.

It was then the door opened and somebody came into the room. Luella was at the far end of it with

Enrico looking at the snuff-box he had found. She turned round and knew unmistakably that this was the Duke of Ingatestone. He was tall, broad-shouldered, and in evening-dress looked quite magnificent, in fact exactly, she thought, as a duke should.

After a moment's silence the Duke said: "I am told that you have come from Italy to see me, but I have not received warning of your arrival."

Luella walked towards him. "I understand a letter is in the post, Your Grace," she said, "but I think it was unlikely to arrive before we did."

The Duke looked towards Enrico, who had turned from the cabinet into which he had been looking to stare at the Duke curiously. Turning back to Luella, the Duke said: "May I ask who you are?"

Stumbling a little because she was nervous, Luella opened her handbag. "I think, Your Grace," she replied, "this letter will explain everything." She drew out the letter that Signor Vecchio had given to her and handed it to the Duke.

He took it from her and said: "I am certainly curious as to why you are here so unexpectedly, but I am sure there must be some perfectly reasonable explanation."

Luella drew in her breath.

Looking at the letter which was addressed to him, the Duke walked to a secretaire. Taking up a letter-opener which lay on it he slit open the envelope.

Luella found herself holding her breath as he drew out a sheet of writing-paper, and something else that was in the envelope. She felt as if her heart would stop beating as she waited for what she knew would be a shock to him. It seemed as if a century passed as the Duke unfolded the writing-paper.

He held what else the envelope had contained in his hand. As he read what was written he stiffened. Then he looked at what the letter had also contained before he asked sharply: "I suppose you are aware of the contents of this letter?"

"N.No . . I was . . only told to bring your . . son to you, and to give . . you the . . letter," Luella answered in a voice that did not sound like her own.

"My son!" the Duke exclaimed scornfully looking at Enrico. "And I presume you are one of the harlots from Vecchio's bawdy house?"

Luella gave a gasp. "Wh.What are you saying?" she stammered.

"Do not try to deceive me," the Duke said. "This is a sheer case of blackmail, and the sooner I turn you and this ridiculous child out of my house, the better."

"I . . I do not . . know what you . . are saying!" Luella exclaimed. "Signor Vecchio asked me to bring your son to England because his mother is dead . . and because I am English."

"You can hardly expect me to believe that is your only reason for coming, if you are part of Vecchio's *maison de plaisir*, as it is called in France, and, doubtless, experienced in blackmail."

The Duke looked down again at the letter in his hand and walked across the room to the window. The light was fading outside, but Luella knew he was staring out as if he thought the setting sun somehow helped him. She was frightened by what he said and the sharp way in which he had spoken. At the same time she was trying to think clearly. Could it be possible that Signor Vecchio was, in fact, blackmailing him? On what grounds could he do so?

It was then that Enrico, aware in his childlike way of the tension in the room, ran to Luella and put his hand in hers. " 'Rico wanna go 'way," he said. "Not lika thees beeg house."

The Duke turned round. "You are quite right," he said, "and it does not like you!" He walked towards Luella and said: "Leave immediately and take the child with you. Go back to where you came from. I will see my solicitors tomorrow." He spoke in such a curt manner that it seemed to Luella that every word cut like a whip.

"I . . I am . . afraid," she said in a small voice, "that it is . . impossible for me . . to leave. The courier who . . brought us here . . has already . . driven away."

"I suppose that was on your instructions," the Duke said in the same tone of voice.

"Certainly not!" Luella protested. "I intended to return to London with him as soon as I had handed over your son to you, as I was requested to do."

"Stop calling him my son!" the Duke ordered. "Does he look like my son? I have never had a son and, I assure you, I have never been married!"

"But . . but Signor Vecchio told me . . that your wife . . whose name was Tia . . had died recently . . and he said that . . as the child was . . yours . . he must join you in . . England and . . take up his . . rightful place." She stumbled over the words, feeling even as she spoke them that they sounded wrong.

"Do you really think that if I had a son he would

look like that?" the Duke asked. "Try and get it into your stupid, scheming head that I have never been married and what we have here is a clever attempt at blackmail!"

"But how . . I do not see . . how?" Luella cried.

"Do not play the innocent with me!" the Duke said sharply. "You are part of this plot, and I have no intention of having anything further to do with you. My solicitors will deal with this. All you have to do is to get out — and quickly!"

"But I cannot do that," Luella gasped. "As I have just said . . it is impossible . . unless you will be kind enough to . . send me in one of your . . carriages."

"I presume you can walk!" the Duke said coldly.

Luella stared at him as if she could hardly believe what she was hearing was true and that he meant what he said.

He looked down again at the paper he held in his hand. "Go back to Vecchio," he said, "and tell him that I will fight him in every court in the country rather than succumb to his filthy tricks."

He stopped speaking to scowl at her, and then went on: "You can also tell him I am well aware that he chose you for your looks, but I am not interested in women of your sort! You should have stayed on the streets where you belong!"

Luella realised how insulting his words were. At the same time, because he was speaking quietly and bitterly, rather than shouting at her, they seemed all the more horrible.

Enrico, who was sensitive, was aware that something unpleasant was happening. He moved closer to

Luella and said with a little whisper: "Let us go 'way.
'Rico wanna go home."

"And that is where you can take him, so get out,
both of you!" It was a command.

Luella turned as if to obey him and walked towards
the door. As she did so she realised the predicament
they were in. They were miles away from civilisation
with no transport, and no means of paying for any. If
she had been alone she might have walked, but she had
Enrico with her. She knew by the way he was clutching
her that the little boy was frightened. With what was
an enormous effort she turned back.

"Please . . Your Grace," she said in a pleading tone,
"please . . listen to me while I . . explain what has
happened."

"I am well aware of what has happened," the Duke
said. "I am holding it here in my hand. This is a
poisonous attempt by a man who ought to have been
hanged years ago, to extract an enormous sum of
money from me in order to prevent a scandal." He
was getting more angry as he went on: "But this time
he has chosen the wrong man! I will fight him in every
court here or in Italy before I will part with a single
penny!"

"And . . what about . . Enrico?" Luella murmured.

"He can go back to the gutter where he came
from and you can do the same!" the Duke replied.
"Doubtless you will find some misguided idiot to
protect you, but you can tell Signor Vecchio that
it will not be me!" Again the way he spoke was so
offensive and at the same time spoken so quietly and
bitterly that every word hurt.

There was silence.

Then Luella said: "I can . . understand that, if, as you say, this whole . . business is a hoax . . and Signor Vecchio is attempting to . . blackmail you . . but I . . Your Grace . . have no wish to play any part in your . . affairs."

She stopped speaking to hold her head high before she continued: "I would like you to know that my name is Luella Hanley . . and my father was a distinguished writer. I became . . involved with Signor Vecchio by chance when I was . . on my way to the . . British Embassy in Milan."

She took a deep breath. "When he asked me to . . oblige him by bringing Enrico to you because his . . mother was dead . . I very foolishly . . I admit . . agreed to do so . . simply because I had no . . money as I had just paid for my father's funeral . . with all we had left in Italy." Her voice died away.

Then taking Enrico by the hand she walked towards the door. "I hope, Your Grace," she said, "we can find a farm-house or a cottage where they will give us shelter for the night . . otherwise . . we shall be obliged . . to sleep under a hedge!" She lifted her chin as she spoke and reaching the door put her hand out towards the handle.

It was then the Duke said: "Wait!!"

Luella did as she was told, but she did not turn round.

"Are you telling me the truth?" he asked.

"I always tell the truth," Luella replied.

"And you really are Richard Hanley's daughter?"

Luella was still. Then she said in a different tone: "You . . you know my . . father's name!"

"I read his book called *The Temples of Greece* only last year." He walked a little way towards her. Then he said: "Do you swear to me on everything you hold holy that Richard Hanley was your father?"

"I swear on the Bible that it is true," Luella said.

The Duke looked at her searchingly. Then he asked: "Can I really believe that you are not connected in any way with that swine Vecchio?"

"What I told you was . . true. I met him by . . chance and because I am English . . he asked me to . . bring this little boy . . to England." Luella was now facing the Duke. She thought he looked deep into her eyes as if he was doubtful that she was telling him the truth, at the same time wanting to believe her.

Then he said: "Very well, Miss Hanley. You had better come and sit down and explain to me from the very beginning how you got yourself involved in this disgraceful mess."

Chapter Four

Reluctantly Luella moved a little further back into the room. Looking down at Enrico, she said: "I think, Your Grace, this little boy is hungry and also tired. Would it be possible for him to have somewhere where he could lie down?"

There was a faint twist to the Duke's lips as he said: "What you are really saying, Miss Hanley, is that you want to stay the night, in which I suppose I shall have to acquiesce."

"As I have already explained," Luella said in a low voice, "we have .. nowhere to go and .. no .. money."

The Duke tugged at the bell that hung beside the mantelpiece. In only a few moments the door was opened and Luella thought the butler had been waiting outside. He was doubtless curious as to what was happening.

"This child, Bates, will be staying the night," the

Duke said, "as will Miss Hanley. Take him to Mrs Moore and ask her to give him something to eat and put him to bed."

"Very good, Your Grace," the butler said.

Luella looked down at Enrico. "I expect you are hungry," she said in Italian. "This gentleman will give you some food, and then find a nice bedroom in which to sleep. I will come to see you as soon as you are in bed."

"Try not forget," Enrico begged.

Luella smiled: "No, of course not, but first they will find you something delicious for supper."

The small boy's dark eyes lit up at this. When the butler held out his hand he put his into it. As if he understood what he must do he said in English: " 'Rico .. verry .. hungr.y. Have .. pain .. in .. tummy."

"Come along then," Bates said, "and I will find you something which will take away the pain and which you will enjoy."

They went from the room and Luella turned towards the Duke. He was standing by the fireplace. As she walked towards him he seemed to be watching her somewhat suspiciously. Because she was still frightened, she said as she reached him: "I am sorry .. I am very .. sorry that .. this has .. happened,"

"You really had no idea what Vecchio was up to?" the Duke asked.

"Certainly not!" Luella replied. "I saw no reason to .. disbelieve him and, to be .. honest, I was .. nervous of travelling .. alone to England without .. somebody with .. me."

"I can understand that," the Duke replied. "Now,

suppose you sit down and start this story from the beginning."

Luella moved to the sofa which faced the fireplace and sat in a corner of it. Because she was still nervous she sat on the edge of the seat and locked her fingers together in her lap.

"You tell me you have no idea what this letter contains," the Duke began, "so I suggest you read it." He held it out to her and Luella took it reluctantly. She had a feeling that the Duke still suspected that she was part of the plot against him. She was afraid that anything she said would involve her more deeply than she was at the moment.

The letter was written in a scholarly hand on expensive white writing-paper. She read:

Your Grace,

This comes to you with your son, who has nowhere to go now that his mother, Tia, is dead and was buried two days ago.

He was born on the 21st February 1875 almost nine months after you left Milan. When you and Tia separated and there was no communication between you, she brought Enrico up at her own expense.

In the years that she has been alone she has incurred some very large debts. These amount, in English money, to approximately half a million pounds.

I shall expect to hear from you concerning them.
I remain,
Yours truly,
Vittorio Vecchio.

When she had read the letter, Luella gave a gasp. "Half a million pounds!" she said. "How could you be expected to pay that?"

"Quite easily," the Duke replied, "if I am to avoid a scandal and have no wish to accept an Italian as my son."

"But if, as you say, you were not married, how can they prove that he is yours?" Luella enquired.

The Duke held out to her another document he had in his hand. As she took it from him she saw that it was a marriage certificate. It was signed by Tia Broletto and Ivor Stone. "So .. you *were* .. married!" she stammered.

"That is a fake," the Duke said. "I admit my signature has been cleverly copied, so I imagine that Tia must have kept a letter of mine. I remember writing to her after I left Italy."

"A fake!" Luella exclaimed. "How is it .. possible they could .. do such a .. thing?"

"Vecchio will do anything that will make him money," the Duke said scornfully. "You cannot have been in Milan very long if you have not heard of him. He is the owner of several disreputable houses, including one which is patronised by many important people and where the girls, I admit, are particularly pretty and carefully chosen!"

He spoke in a sharp, cold voice and Luella asked somewhat tentatively: "Is .. is that .. where you .. met Tia?"

"I was on a mission," the Duke explained, "with an extremely boring general and it was a relief to get away from the official conferences and dinner-parties.

I went to what I suppose you could call the 'red light district' to seek amusement."

Because she understood what he was saying Luella blushed. She also turned her face away as if she did not want to ask any more questions.

However, as if he wished her to know the truth, the Duke went on: "Tia was very attractive and I imagine about the same age as yourself. I was in Milan for a week and saw her every evening when I was off duty."

He paused and went on, his voice sharpening: "There was no question of there being anything permanent in our relationship. She had been well-trained by Vecchio in knowing how to make a man enjoy himself without any thought of responsibilities."

Luella did not say anything and the Duke continued: "Even in Italy, where it is accepted that such men have a place in the night life of a city, Vecchio is considered an evil influence."

"I . . I thought there . . was something . . wrong about him," Luella said, "but . . I did not know . . what it . . was."

"And yet you trusted him."

"He seemed surprised that I was alone when I was looking at the Cathedral and offered to escort me back to the hotel where I had been staying with my father."

"You are fortunate that he did not take you to one of his 'mansions' and drug you," the Duke said. "After that, I am told, there is no escape."

Luella gave a little cry. "So that is . . what he . . intended! I realise now why when he offered me some .. coffee I was suddenly .. frightened and .. refused it."

"Very wisely so," the Duke said. "If you had drunk the coffee you would certainly not be here now."

"I .. never .. thought of it being .. drugged!" Luella murmured.

"Then you must be very foolish or very innocent," the Duke said sharply. "Surely you know better than to accept a drink from a stranger in an Italian city, when you look like you do?"

Luella twisted her fingers together. "I .. I know it wa.s.wrong of me .. but he seemed fatherly and .. k.kind .. and I had just .. come from the Cathedral .. where I had gone to .. pray after m.my .. father was .. buried."

She gave a little sob as she added: "I was .. alone and thinking .. how uncomfortable and .. embarrassing it would be to have .. to go to the .. British Embassy .. and say I had .. no money."

"How could you possibly have got yourself into such a situation," the Duke asked, "where you had no money and were alone in a city like Milan?"

"Papa was taken .. seriously ill .. and for ten days lay unconscious. Although I called in the best doctors, they could do .. nothing for him .. but they were .. expensive. Then he .. d.died without .. ever .. speaking to me again!"

There was a pathetic note in her voice and the Duke's voice was kinder as he said: "I can understand your predicament, Miss Hanley, but you should have gone straight to the British Embassy."

"That .. is what I .. intended to do," Luella said,

"and I cannot imagine . . how I was so . . s.stupid as to . . agree to what Signor Vecchio . . suggested."

"I am sure he was very persuasive," the Duke said sarcastically. "He has had a great deal of experience in picking up attractive young women at railway stations, coaching inns, and of course outside the Cathedral."

Luella looked down at her hands. She was thinking that the Duke had every right to rebuke her, just as her father and mother would have done. Once again she could see the strange look in Signor Vecchio's eyes and the smile on his lips when he suggested giving her coffee. She realised now that it was only because they had been interrupted by Father Sebastian that he had changed his mind.

When she thought of it, she remembered how he had spoken to her in a very different tone when he came back into the room. She gave a sudden cry. "I have thought of something!" she said. "Something, Your Grace, which concerns . . you!"

"What is it?" the Duke asked.

She thought he did not sound particularly hopeful and she said: "I think, if I am not mistaken, that when I was in the Cathedral, I saw the priest, whom Signor Vecchio obviously knew, called Father Sebastian, looking at the marriage register that had just been signed by a bride and bridegroom."

The Duke stared at her. "Are you suggesting that he was tearing out the certificate we have here?"

"I am almost sure of it!" Luella said, "I watched him go into the chapel just beside me." She thought for a moment and then went on: "The servers were carrying away the chalice and the wine. He stood for some time in front of the register with his back to me. When the servers returned, he hurried away, almost knocking them down."

The Duke was listening intently and she paused for breath before she continued: "I thought he looked a surprisingly rough, unpleasant sort of man to be a priest, and when he appeared in Signor Vecchio's office, he shouted in Italian: 'I've found it! I've found it!'"

The Duke looked puzzled. "You say you saw this man, Father Sebastian, in the Cathedral," he said. "Then he came into Vecchio's office. That seems unlikely."

"It was him! I am sure it was the same man!" Luella said. "Signor Vecchio quickly said in Italian: 'Look out! We are not alone', and hurried him out of the room."

"Then what happened?" the Duke enquired.

"I was alone for some time," Luella answered, "then Signor Vecchio came back and suggested that I take Enrico to England."

The Duke drew in his breath. "I am beginning to understand how it was all worked out," he said. "Vecchio must have learned that I had become the Duke of Ingatestone."

"He knew about you. He told me he had read of the disaster to your family in the Italian newspapers."

The Duke nodded. "And when Tia died, he knew this was his opportunity to make a great deal of money by pretending the child was mine."

"I felt it was odd when we picked him up from a poor-looking house," Luella said. "Signor Vecchio told me to wait in the carriage when he went inside to collect the little boy. He had said that Tia was so charming and popular that everyone had wept at her funeral. I thought it strange that she should be living in such a hovel."

"It may be her child, it may not," the Duke said. "It could be that Vecchio merely found a weapon with which to blackmail me."

"It should be easy to find that out," Luella said.

The Duke gave a laugh that had no humour in it. "That may be true, but, knowing Vecchio, he will have covered his tracks. He is a past-master at intrigue, and of course at blackmail! I was warned about him by everyone I met in Italy."

He sighed before he said: "They admitted however that his 'houses' were comparable to the very best in Paris, and the girls whom he obtained from many different countries were superior to anything that could be found anywhere else in Europe!"

"Can you not prove that the marriage certificate is a .. forgery?" Luella asked.

The Duke was still holding it in his hand and now he looked down at it. "It has been very skilfully done by an expert, I should imagine, who of course will be well known to Vecchio."

"I .. I must have .. seen him!" Luella exclaimed.

"What do you mean?" the Duke asked.

"We were waiting at the hotel next to the station, and we got there far too early, which seemed to me strange."

She paused a moment to think, and then said: "A man came into the room and Signor Vecchio was obviously expecting him. They sat so far away from us that I could not hear what they said. But the man handed something to Signor Vecchio, who gave him a large sum of money."

"That would have been the forged certificate!" the Duke exclaimed. "The blank which the priest had removed from the marriage register. What you have told me, Miss Hanley, has been very, very helpful, but we still have to prove it to be the truth."

"How are . . we to do . . that?" Luella asked.

"I am not certain," the Duke answered, "but your information will be of vital importance." He glanced down again at the marriage certificate. "I see that the priest who signed it is called 'Sebastian' and the marriage is supposed to have taken place seven years ago. I suppose he got the same man who is now helping Vecchio to blackmail me."

Luella had not noticed this when she had looked at the marriage certificate. Now she bent forward to look closer at it, and the Duke held it up in front of her. The name was somehow obscured, but it was undoubtedly Sebastian. "If Father Sebastian signed this seven years ago," Luella said, "perhaps by now he has retired, or else was dismissed."

"That is certainly a possibility," the Duke agreed, "and he would therefore be grateful to be cut in for a large sum of money, such as Vecchio hopes to extort from me."

He stopped for a moment, and then went on: "He believes I will pay it to prevent a scandal and prevent me too from becoming the father of an Italian child who I could never accept as my heir." Now there was an angry note in the Duke's voice, as if even to speak of it was repulsive to him.

It seemed to Luella they were caught up in a web of intrigue and evil which enveloped them both. There apparently was to be no escape and she suddenly began to feel sorry for the Duke. He was young, he was handsome. It must have been very exciting for him suddenly to have become a man of such great importance. This plot would be a bombshell which would shatter his contentment as surely as if somebody had plunged a dagger into his heart.

"I am .. sorry .. terribly sorry," she said aloud.

"I can only say," the Duke replied, "that if I am to be involved in anything so unpleasant and disgraceful, I am fortunate to have you to help me." He shook his head before saying: "The child might have arrived simply with a courier, or perhaps with some Italian who was demanding a first instalment of the money Vecchio is trying to extort from me."

"I want to .. help you .. and I will .. help you in .. every way .. I can," Luella said.

"Then what I want you to do tomorrow," the Duke answered, "after you have rested, is to write down everything you can remember about this unpleasant business from start to finish."

"Yes .. of course I will .. do that," Luella promised.

Unexpectedly the Duke smiled, "As your father's daughter, you should be very eloquent about it."

"Did you really enjoy my father's book on the Greek temples?" Luella asked.

"I found it fascinating!" the Duke replied. "I went

to Greece for a holiday, and I was enthralled by Delphi and of course the Parthenon." He smiled at her as he continued: "There was so much more I wanted to know that the guides could not tell me, but when your father's book was published, it answered all my questions."

"I am glad . . so very glad," Luella murmured.

"Has he written anything else?" the Duke enquired.

"He was just finishing a book on the cathedrals and churches of Europe, which is why we were in Milan," Luella explained. "He wanted to see St. Peter's in Rome, then the Cathedral in Milan."

"If he had nearly completed the book," the Duke said, "that means that you must finish it for him."

Luella looked startled: "I never thought of it."

"But of course it is something you must do," the Duke said. "If his new book is as good as *The Temples of Greece* then you owe it to him and to his readers to see that it is published."

"I have it with me," Luella said, "and I will take it to the publishers as soon as I return to London." She made a little gesture with her hands as she said: "I should have thought of that myself, but it was such a . . shock when Papa died . . leaving me all . . alone. I could . . only wonder where I . . should go."

"But you meant to come to England," the Duke replied, "as of course your father's relatives are here."

"I have to find them first," Luella said simply. She thought the Duke looked puzzled and she explained: "Papa has been to England only twice since he married Mama, and I am not certain which of his relatives are still alive, or even if they would be prepared to look after me."

The Duke stared at her. "Are you telling me," he asked, "that you came back to England with no money and no idea of where you could go?"

"I thought I would call on Papa's publishers who might know more about my family than I did. If they could help me, I do know the name of the village where Papa's parents used to live and where Papa was brought up."

"Surely that could be very dangerous?" the Duke suggested. "You have got yourself into one difficult situation, Miss Hanley, by moving about alone. It is certainly something you must not do again."

Luella smiled. "I am afraid there is no alternative. My parents were constantly on the move, exploring different parts of the world. As we never settled for long in any one place, I have no friends." She sighed and added: "I realise now of course that it was silly of me not to have asked Papa about his relatives."

"I am sure you will be able to find them," the Duke said confidently. "I will ask my secretary tomorrow morning to see what he can do." He smiled before he went on: "Your father made a name for himself with *The Temples of Greece*. There must be people around who would be only too delighted to help his daughter."

"I hope so," Luella replied, "for I have no wish to starve to death!"

"Of course not," the Duke agreed, "but if your father's new book is published, I am sure they will advance you some money. In fact I will make sure that they do so."

"It is very kind of you to . . say that," Luella said, "especially when I have brought you so much . . trouble." She saw the Duke's eyes harden and said quickly: "But you do believe now that I had . . no part in this . . deception?"

"Of course I believe you, now that I have had time to talk to you," the Duke replied. "But you had a very narrow escape, Miss Hanley, from being drugged and finding yourself in a dreadful place from which you could never escape."

He stopped speaking to look at her very seriously: "You must never again — and I mean never again — walk about the streets of a foreign city alone, or get into conversation with a strange man — however pleasant he may appear to be."

"It was . . very, very . . foolish . . of me," Luella admitted, "and I know now that Papa would have been very . . angry indeed, if he . . knew what . . happened."

"I think that your father would have been grateful that, by the mercy of God, you escaped," the Duke said, "and at least for tonight, at any rate, you can sleep without being afraid."

"Does that mean you will allow me to stay here?" Luella asked. "Oh, thank you . . thank you. I thought the courier was going to give me some . . money which Signor Vecchio had promised." She gave a deep sigh and added: "But he drove away without telling me he was going to do so, and now I think it was Signor Vecchio who intended to make sure that I should be left .. penniless."

"I am quite certain that is what he planned," the Duke said. "The man is an evil monster, and that is why, Miss Hanley, we have to fight him with every weapon we have at our disposal."

As the Duke finished speaking, he looked at the clock over the mantelpiece. "It is growing late," he said, "and I am sure you are hungry. I hope you will give me the pleasure of dining with me."

Luella rose from the sofa. "If you are .. sure that is what .. you want."

"I was dining alone," the Duke said, "because I have been very busy all day organising improvements to the estate. I expect by this time your luggage will have gone upstairs and I would like, if it is possible, to put back dinner for no more than twenty minutes."

Luella gave a little laugh. "I can be quicker than that."

"Very well," the Duke smiled. "That is a challenge!" He walked to the door and opened it.

Luella was not surprised to see that Bates, the butler, was standing just outside. "I was waiting to tell Your Grace," he said, as the Duke appeared, "that the little boy has eaten a large meal, and Mrs Moore has taken him upstairs to bed."

"I promised I would go up and say goodnight to him," Luella said.

The Duke turned to the butler. "Take Miss Hanley upstairs," he said, "and order dinner to be ready at eight-thirty."

"Very good, Your Grace." The butler walked ahead and Luella followed him.

When they reached the first floor she saw that the housekeeper was already there waiting for her. There was no mistaking the black frock with its silk apron and a silver chatelaine falling from an elderly woman's waist. Luella's mother had often told her how the housekeepers in the big houses in England were dressed, She had laughed at the number of servants employed by the nobility.

"Well now, here you are, Miss," Mrs Moore said as Luella appeared. "The little boy was asking for you, an' I don't think he'll settle until you say goodnight to him."

"That is just what I am going to do," Luella answered.

Mrs Moore took her to a room which was only a short way along the passage. It was a large bedroom with a large bed and Enrico looked lost in it. When Luella appeared he held out his arms. " 'Rico in beeg sheep," he said in English, "an' I wanna you come with me."

"I think you must go to sleep in this big ship," Luella said, "and tomorrow I will tell you a story all about it."

"Now! Now!" the little boy pleaded.

Luella shook her head. "You have had a delicious supper," she said, "and I am hungry."

"Choc'late cake! 'Rico have choc'late cake!"

"That is what I hope I shall have too," Luella answered. "So go to sleep now and you shall have your story in the morning."

She kissed Enrico and realised as she did so that he was very tired. He cuddled down against the pillow saying: " 'Rico .. in beeg .. sheep sailing .. over sea."

"That is right," Luella said, "and you can pretend the waves are moving underneath you." His eyelids were drooping, and she knew he would be asleep almost before she left the room.

She was relieved to find that she was in the room next door. She knew that if Enrico was frightened in the night she would hear him. Some of her clothes had been unpacked, and she washed quickly and put on one of her prettiest evening-gowns. It was one her father had bought for her in Rome. Because it had been packed last it was not as creased as it might otherwise have been.

She was used to dressing quickly to set off on one of her father's expeditions or to see something about which he had just been told. She was therefore downstairs again in less than the twenty minutes. Bates showed her into the drawing-room where the Duke was waiting.

As she walked towards the Duke he said: "Excellent! I feel sure that your father's training makes you punctual where most women are exceedingly unpunctual."

"I was just thinking of how often I have had to pack up at short notice everything I possess and set out for a strange country, a mountain, or an ancient building."

"An excellent training for any young woman!" the Duke observed. He spoke rather like a schoolmaster, but his eyes were twinkling.

"Dinner is served, Your Grace!" the butler announced from the doorway.

"If you are not hungry, I am!" the Duke said to Luella.

"I feel like Enrico. I have a hole in my tummy," Luella said without thinking. Then she blushed because it sounded too intimate to stay to a stranger.

The Duke however laughed. "Is the little Italian all right?" he enquired.

"He is delighted with his bed, which he thinks is a big ship," Luella said. "He really is a dear little boy, and has been very good, considering we had a very long journey and an extremely tiring one." The Duke did not answer. She thought perhaps it was embarrassing if she talked about Enrico.

And yet she knew there would have to be some decision made about him. The question was whether he should be sent back to Italy, or allowed to stay in England.

She remembered the sordid house from which he had come. The Duke had told her a great deal about Signor Vecchio. Now it occurred to her that he would not care what happened to Enrico once he had served his purpose.

'What can I do about him?" she asked herself. She knew it was another problem on her shoulders besides her own.

Chapter Five

To her surprise Luella slept peacefully, and when she awoke it was later than she expected. She got out of bed and hurried into Enrico's bedroom to find that he was still asleep. It was with a feeling of relief that she went back to her own room. She would have felt guilty if Enrico had wanted her in the night and she had not heard him calling her.

The sun was pouring through the window. She stood looking out at the trees and the lake, thinking what a picture it made. It was exactly as she had expected England to look.

When she was dressed she found Enrico was awake and she helped him to dress. Then they went downstairs for breakfast. Luella expected to have to apologise to the Duke. When she entered the breakfast-room, however, Bates told her that His Grace had gone riding.

Enrico pricked up his ears. " 'Rico – ride," he said, "on beeg . . horse."

"I tell you what we will do," Luella said. "We will go after breakfast to the stables where we will look at the big horses, but I think you will have to grow much larger before you can ride them."

Enrico was so excited that he chatted away in Italian because it was easier for him. He explained that he wanted to ride big horses so that he could jump very big hedges. Because he seemed so happy, Luella let him talk in his own language.

When breakfast was finished, they went to the stables. It was a warm day and there was no need for coats, nor, as far as Luella was concerned, a hat. The sun shone on her golden hair. Because she was so unselfconscious she had no idea that the grooms and stable lads watched her admiringly. They paraded some of the horses in the yard so that she and Enrico could see them better.

Then to Enrico's delight, the head groom lifted him up onto the back of one of the horses. " 'Rico riding!" he shouted. " 'Rico riding on verry beeg horse!"

As his voice echoed round the stables the Duke came into the yard. He was riding a magnificent black stallion. Luella felt embarrassed. She was afraid the Duke might think they had presumed on their precarious position as his guests in going to the stables.

To her relief, however, when he dismounted he walked up to her and said: "I imagine that, as you have been all over the world with your father, you can ride?"

Luella laughed. "Anything!" she claimed. "From a reluctant mule to a yak."

"I could provide you with something better than that," the Duke said, "but I have decided that we must leave for London this afternoon after an early luncheon."

"Y.yes . . of course," Luella said in a low voice. She suddenly thought how wrong it was for her and Enrico to be enjoying themselves. They were laughing while the Duke was beset with the danger of a scandal.

Enrico, protesting, was lifted off the horse. Luella, leading him by the hand, started to walk back to the Castle.

" 'Rico wanna . . ride . . rida beeg . . horse!" he insisted.

"Perhaps you will be able to do that another day," Luella said. "We are going to drive behind some very big horses this afternoon."

" 'Rico ride!" he said firmly.

It was easier not to argue.

When they went into the Castle the Duke said to the butler: "Tell Mrs Moore to have Miss Hanley's luggage ready so that we can leave at one o'clock."

"Very good, Your Grace," Bates replied.

They went into a room on the ground floor which overlooked the garden. Like every other room Luella had been in, there was fine furniture and pictures by Old Masters on the walls. She thought wistfully that she would never have time to see them, nor to explore the Castle, as she longed to do. She was just about to ask if there was time to see the library before luncheon, when Bates announced:

"The Dowager Marchioness of Dumbleton, Your Grace!"

An elderly woman, very smartly dressed, came into the room. "Aunt Anne!" the Duke exclaimed. "This is a surprise!"

"I am on my way to London," the newcomer said, "and I thought I would drop in to see you."

"Then of course you must stay to luncheon," the Duke said.

"I was hoping you would ask me," his Aunt smiled.

Then she looked in surprise at Luella and the Duke said hastily: "Let me introduce Miss Hanley, whose father wrote *The Temples of Greece*, which I am sure you have read."

The Marchioness held out her hand. At the same time she was looking at Enrico. "And who is the little boy?" she enquired.

Luella knew that the Duke was thinking quickly, but there was a pause before he said: "He is the son of a friend of mine in Italy, who has recently died. She has sent him to England, asking if I would find a suitable school for him."

The Marchioness laughed. "Really, Ivor, people do seem to expect you to do the strangest things for them!"

"That is what I thought myself," the Duke replied.

"You must ask the Italian Ambassador to help you," the Marchioness went on. "I sat next to him at dinner at Marlborough House last week, and thought him a charming man."

"That is a very good idea, Aunt Anne," the Duke

answered. "I will get in touch with him as soon as I reach London this afternoon."

"So you are going to London, too!" the Marchioness exclaimed. "I knew you were here for a night or two, but I thought you were *alone*."

She accentuated the last word slightly, and the Duke said quickly: "Miss Hanley appeared unexpectedly yesterday evening, and you will not be surprised to learn that the letter announcing her arrival has not been delivered and is probably already lost!"

"It does not surprise me in the least!" the Marchioness agreed.

"I will just go and see about luncheon," the Duke said, "and I suppose your coachman will go round to the yard?"

"He knows the way," the Marchioness answered.

The Duke went from the room. Luella thought he was looking annoyed at being questioned as to why she was in the Castle unchaperoned. Enrico was searching among the cabinets to see if he could find a ship like the one he had found yesterday. The Marchioness, obviously curious, sat down on a sofa. "Come and tell me all about yourself," she said.

Luella, somewhat nervously, went and sat down beside her. "I do not think I have seen you here before," the Marchioness continued.

"I have been living abroad," Luella said, "and have only just come from Italy."

"So that is where you must have met my nephew," the Marchioness said. "Of course everything is very different for him now from what it was before." She glanced around the room before she added: "As I expect you know, he inherited his position quite unexpectedly, and he must now adjust himself to a new life."

"I understand that," Luella agreed.

"And of course," the Marchioness went on, "we are all hoping he will marry, settle down, and produce a son. That is essential if the family is to continue as it has done for four hundred years."

Luella did not say anything and the Marchioness, as if choosing her words, said: "It is obviously extremely important for him to choose a Duchess who will fill a very important position in the way that is expected of her."

The way the Marchioness spoke told Luella only too clearly what she was pointing out. As the daughter of a mere writer, it would be a mistake for her to 'set her sights' on anyone as important as the Duke of Ingatestone. The Marchioness lowered her voice as she said: "I can tell you confidentially, Miss Hanley, that Her Majesty the Queen is anxious that my nephew should marry someone of whom she approves. In fact, she already has someone in mind."

Luella was wondering how she could say, without sounding rude, that she had no pretensions about marrying him. She realised this was what the older woman assumed she was trying to do.

It was then the Duke returned to say: "Everything is arranged, Aunt Anne, and I know you will want to have luncheon early, so that you can travel to London while it is still light."

Luella rose to her feet. "I will go and see that

Enrico's things have been packed," she said. She took the little boy, who had been quietly playing with some priceless snuff-boxes, out of the room with her. She noticed how carefully he handled them. It was, she thought, characteristic of his Italian blood that he appreciated beautiful things and was not clumsy with them.

As soon as they had left the room the Marchioness said to the Duke: "Surely, Ivor, that young woman has not been staying her unchaperoned? It would be a great mistake."

"I know that, Aunt Anne," the Duke agreed, "but unfortunately, as I have already told you, the letter announcing her arrival has been delayed. When she got here late last night I could hardly magic a chaperon out of the air!"

"It is something which must not occur again!" the Marchioness said sharply. "And this must certainly not be talked about." She paused before she added: "If the girl has an ambitious father and mother, they might accuse you of destroying her reputation, and you know what that would mean!"

"My dear Aunt Anne," the Duke said, "you are 'making a mountain out of a molehill'. As it happens, Miss Hanley's parents are both dead."

"But you must be aware," the Marchioness went on, "how poor Lord Worchester got caught in a most despicable trap merely by talking alone with a young woman in the garden." She paused a moment and then continued: "Her mother pleaded with the Prince of Wales to force him into marriage as the only reparation."

"I heard about that," the Duke replied, "and I thought myself that Worchester was rather wet about the whole affair."

The Marchioness threw up her hands. "My dear, what was he to do when the Prince of Wales was telling him he had to behave like a gentleman?"

"I assure you, you need not worry on my account," the Duke said firmly.

At the same time he understood why the Marchioness was apprehensive. It had not struck him last night that he should somehow acquire a chaperon in the shape of a married woman for Luella. Now he thought of it, he realised he should have asked his secretary if there was someone available on the estate. But he had been so appalled by Vecchio's flagrant threat to blackmail him that he had not thought of anything else.

The Marchioness put her hand on his arm. "You must remember, dear boy," she said, "that you are not only a very attractive young man, but also the Duke of Ingatestone. You are expected to keep up your position and also provide an heir to follow you."

"You do not have to worry, Aunt Anne," the Duke protested. "I am still 'feeling my feet' as the owner of this magnificent estate, and I have no intention of getting married until I am very much older."

"We shall have to see what Her Majesty the Queen has to say about that!" the Marchioness observed.

The Duke gave her a sharp look, but thought it would be a mistake to ask her to explain herself. It was with a sense of relief that he realised that Bates was bringing the champagne which he had ordered.

* * *

Upstairs Luella found that Mrs Moore had already had her clothes put back into her trunk. Enrico's small belongings had also been packed. "Thank you very much, Mrs Moore," Luella said.

She then realised she was expected to tip the two maids who had waited on her. She went to her handbag and found the few Italian coins given to her by Signor Vecchio. She divided them between the two women, apologising for the fact that it was not English money. She explained that she had had no time to change it when she arrived in England.

"That's all right, Miss," one of them said, "an' I thinks I'll jus' keep mine for luck!"

"And I hope that is what it will bring you," Luella said. She was thinking however that she now had no money left – literally not a penny. She could only hope that the Duke was right and her father's publishers would be delighted at the idea of having a new book from him. Then perhaps they would advance her some money.

"Please, God .. let them be .. generous," she prayed. She knew she would feel embarrassed at having to ask the Duke to lend her money. But she realised that when she reached London she would have to find somewhere to stay.

Enrico had washed his hands and now she took him downstairs. She listened to him talking excitedly about riding until luncheon was ready. It was only a light meal, but Enrico obviously enjoyed every mouthful.

Luella however was worrying again about the future and especially what she could do about tonight.

She was well aware that even if the Duke invited her
to stay in his London house, she could not do so after
what the Marchioness had hinted to her. "What am I
.. to do?" she asked herself. "What *am* I to .. do?"

There was no answer. She could only think how
overwhelmingly grand the dining-room of the huge
castle was. The superb silver ornaments on the table,
the butler and footmen in attendance, bore no com-
parison to her own situation.

The Marchioness left first, driving away in a smart,
closed carriage drawn by two grey horses. There were
a coachman and a footman on the box. A lady's-maid
sat inside facing the Marchioness with her back to the
horses.

The Duke waved his Aunt goodbye, as his travelling
carriage moved up to the front door. It was up to date
and roomy and, at the same time, built for speed.
It was drawn by four perfectly matched chestnuts,
and Luella knew it would be very exciting to drive
behind them.

There was plenty of room for Enrico who was
looking thrilled at the sight of the horses. When Luella
would have put him between her and the Duke he
suggested Enrico should sit outside. He explained that
he would see better and it was where he had always
preferred to be when he was a boy. Luella thought it
was kind of him to think of it.

As she sat down beside the Duke she felt a strange
little tremor run through her because she was so close
to him. He was looking magnificent in a whipcord
riding coat, and with a tall hat slightly to one side
of his head. He was undoubtedly the most handsome

man she had ever seen. She knew as they set off down the drive that this was something she would remember for the rest of her life.

The carriage was carrying them faster than she had ever gone before. It was not hampered by the luggage, which was following them in a brake. Also in the brake were the Duke's valet together with several other servants. Luella thought they must have come down from London with him and were now returning.

The chestnut team soon passed the Marchioness's carriage. They were out of sight of the brake almost before they left the village.

"Will you be going to see the Italian Ambassador?" Luella said to the Duke.

"I have already sent a groom to London asking him to call on me as soon as he possibly can," the Duke replied. Luella looked surprised and the Duke explained: "When my Aunt mentioned him, I thought I would be wise to consult him about my problem before I approach my solicitors."

He paused a moment and then went on: "Once it is in their hands, it may easily, however discreet they may be, be talked about by the wrong people." There was silence before he added: "As this is an Italian menace, it should be part of the Ambassador's responsibility to see that I am not blackmailed in this diabolical manner by one of his countrymen."

"That seems to be a good idea," Luella agreed.

"I thought you would think so," the Duke answered. "Therefore the quicker we can get to London, the better."

Because they were going so fast, it was difficult to talk. In fact, they drove in silence until half-way there they stopped at a posting inn. The Duke had his own horses waiting for him. They were another well-matched team, but this time jet black, with the exception of a white star on their noses. They were fresh, frisky and moved even more swiftly, Luella thought, than the chestnuts.

When she remembered how long it had taken her when driving to the Castle with Mr Drago, she could hardly believe it when they reached the outskirts of London.

As they moved into the traffic which slowed their pace, she said in a hesitating voice: "I .. I do not .. like to .. bother Your Grace .. but where will .. Enrico and I .. stay the night?"

"You are going to stay at my house in Park Lane," the Duke replied, "and so that my Aunt will not be shocked, you will be provided with a chaperon." Luella waited and he went on: "I sent a message to my London secretary to find one, and I expect it will be his wife, who is a very charming woman."

Luella could only give a sigh of relief. Now she need not humiliate herself by having to ask him for some money. Instead she said in a low voice: "Thank you .. thank you very .. much! I am so .. sorry to be such a .. nuisance."

"You are nothing of the sort!" the Duke replied. "You have promised to help me, and it is absolutely essential that you personally tell the Italian Ambassador exactly what you told me. Then we can leave him to find a solution."

Luella thought she should be very grateful to the Marchioness for having suggested the Ambassador. At the same time, she was worried about Enrico. She could not help thinking about the sordid street from which Signor Vecchio had collected him. Yet he looked in no way neglected. The clothes he wore were expensive and in good condition.

She wanted to ask the Duke what he thought had happened to the boy before his mother died. It seemed unlikely that he would have lived in one of Signor Vecchio's houses. Perhaps Tia had had a flat of her own. But she knew she would not talk to the Duke about Tia without feeling embarrassed. She just had to wonder to herself, and find no answer to the questions that were in her mind.

As they drew up outside the Duke's large house in Park Lane, he said: "I am certain I have broken the record! It has taken me only three-and-a-half hours to get here. I have never done it as quickly as that before."

"That be true, Y'Grace," the groom agreed, who had got down from his seat at the back of the travelling carriage.

"Then I am very pleased with myself!" the Duke said. "Now, see that the horses are given a good feed, because they deserve it."

The groom grinned. "Oi'll do that, Y'Grace." He touched his hat respectfully as the Duke and Luella walked into the house.

There was another butler, white-haired and not unlike Bates. There were also six footmen in attendance. "What we want is champagne, Hewitt," the Duke said. "I have broken the record coming here, and it is something I have been hoping to do for some time."

"Congratulations, Y'Grace," the butler replied, "an' there's champagne on ice in Your Grace's study."

The Duke walked ahead. Luella found herself in a very attractive room at the back of the house which overlooked a garden. There were shelves of books which Luella knew her father would have enjoyed reading. The Duke gave her a glass of champagne and the butler brought some lemonade for Enrico. " 'Rico want .. go back to .. beeg horses," he was saying.

"Perhaps tomorrow," Luella said, "His Grace will let you go and look at the horses he has in the mews." She glanced at the Duke as she spoke. She thought that once again she was imposing on his good nature.

"He shall certainly see the horses," he replied, "and if we have to be in London long, as I suspect we will, I will hire a pony that he can ride."

Luella was astonished. At the same time, she could only say: "Thank .. you! Thank you very .. much!"

It was later, when she had washed and changed her gown, that she came downstairs alone. A young housemaid had been told to look after Enrico. He was playing with some toys which had apparently belonged to one of the late Duke's sons. Luella found the Duke alone in the study and she said to him: "Could I please speak to you about Enrico?"

"Of course," he replied. He had been sitting at his desk when she entered, studying a pile of documents and letters. He rose and walked towards the fireplace.

"I am worried," Luella began in a small voice, "in case the Ambassador, when he learns . . why he came to . . England, simply sends him back to Milan . . and to Signor Vecchio."

The Duke did not say anything, and she went on quickly: "You have . . told me how wicked and evil he is! I am sure therefore . . that he has no real interest in . . the little boy . . and perhaps . . now that his mother is dead . . he will be . . ill-treated . . or left to . . s.starve."

Still the Duke did not say anything and she looked at him pleadingly as she said: "I . . I could not . . bear that to happen and I would rather . . look after him . . myself . . which I can do if my father's book is . . published." She paused a moment before she finished: "I shall then have . . some money . . but perhaps in the meantime . . I could . . borrow a little from you . . and I promise I will . . pay you back."

The Duke raised his eyebrows. "Do you really intend to saddle yourself with an Italian child who, if you are telling me the truth, you had never seen until a few days ago?"

"I *am* telling you . . the truth," Luella said. "Enrico is a dear little boy and he has been well brought up. I could not . . bear him to be . . unhappy. He has very . . good manners . . and at table he behaves as well as . . you or I do."

"What you are implying," the Duke said in a hard voice, "is that his father, whoever he may be, must have been a gentleman."

"I suppose our . . instincts and . . whatever qualities we are born with show themselves as soon as we . .

begin to .. walk and talk," Luella suggested. "I ..
therefore .. believe that what .. you have just said
is .. true."

"And you really want to undertake the task of
bringing the child up yourself," the Duke asked,
"despite the fact that he is not of your nationality?"

"It will .. not be.easy," Luella answered, "but it is
something I am .. ready to do .. rather than let him
go back to .. Signor Vecchio .. now that I know how
.. wicked he is!"

"And you expect me to let that happen?" the
Duke asked.

Luella looked at him. "You mean .. you will not
.. allow the Ambassador to .. send him back?"

"I would not send any living creature to a man I so
utterly despise, and who I think is the Devil himself!"
the Duke said sharply.

Luella gave a cry of relief. "I am so glad .. so very
glad! It would be a crime .. a terrible crime!"

"And yet it was a crime you thought I might
commit!" the Duke persisted.

"I hoped and .. prayed you would not," Luella said
simply.

To her surprise the Duke smiled. "Between us,"
he said, "I am sure we can contrive that the young
Italian one way or another, has the chance of a
decent life."

"Oh, thank you .. thank you! You are wonderful
to be so understanding!" Luella cried. "I was .. so
afraid you would .. refuse to .. help me."

"I have not said that I will allow you to look after
him," the Duke pointed out. "You are very young,

Luella, and very beautiful. Just as I have to think of Enrico's future, I have to think of yours."

"No!" Luella said fiercely. "I have to look after myself. I am sure if Papa's book is published I shall have enough money to do that."

"I will send for your father's publishers tomorrow," the Duke promised. "It is too late now, and anyway, we are all tired after such a long journey."

"Now that you have been so kind," Luella answered, "I feel as if I had wings on my feet and could fly into the sky, or dance in the garden under the trees!"

The Duke laughed. "That is something I would very much like to see you do. In fact, if it were not that my Aunt Anne would violently disapprove, I would take you out to supper this evening at Romano's or somewhere where we could dance."

"That would be . . marvellous!" Luella exclaimed.

The Duke shook his head. "After the lecture she gave me this morning about allowing you to stay in the Castle unchaperoned, I can assure you that my other relations, like my Aunt, would be horrified at the idea of my dancing alone with a lady, unchaperoned in any restaurant!"

"Then I am sure they would be deeply shocked at some of the places I have been to with my father and mother," Luella said. "We have been to palaces in India, and in Egypt, where the women danced in an exotic manner which Papa later wrote about, but which was considered very unsuitable for me."

"Then why did they take you?" the Duke enquired.

"Because they did not want to leave me alone at an hotel or in a tent, or wherever they were staying at the time!" She stopped and sighed before she went on: "But Mama said that when I was taken to the Tiznit dancers, who as you know are the most exciting and sensational in the whole of the East, I was tired and slept all through it."

The Duke laughed. "I can see, Luella," he said, "that you have had a very cosmopolitan education."

"It has certainly taken place in a great many countries," Luella answered. She was aware that he had called her by her Christian name. She thought it was because he looked upon her as a child to be protected. He obviously looked upon her rather as he did Enrico.

"I tell you what we will do," the Duke said. "Tomorrow I will invite some friends to join us, and I will take a box at the theatre."

"I would love that!" Luella cried. "Oh, thank you .. thank you!"

"Of course we may have to go to something rather dull and respectable," the Duke said. "But I hope you will manage to stay awake!"

Luella realised he was teasing her and she said: "It is the most exciting thing that has ever happened to me, so please do not forget."

"I will try not to," the Duke promised but his eyes were twinkling.

He had been thinking while he was talking that it was very unusual to find someone so enthusiastic and so full of life. He had been far too wise to associate with young girls whose Mamas were trying to force him up the aisle. But unlike Luella, they giggled and blushed if a man so much as spoke to them.

Luella had lived a very different sort of life. He knew it would be interesting to talk to her of her adventures in various parts of the world. Also he would like to show her parts of England she had not seen before.

Then he remembered that the one purpose of keeping Luella and the small boy with him was to save himself from being blackmailed. He thought how horrified his relatives would be if they became aware of the appalling difficulty he was in at this moment. They would be furious at the idea of his having to part with an enormous sum of money which would undoubtedly cripple the estate. They would be even more appalled at the thought of a scandal when he had so recently come into the title. He did not realise that he was echoing the question that was in Luella's mind as he asked: "What shall I do? What the devil shall I do?"

Chapter Six

Luella put Enrico to bed. When she had done so he flung his arms round her neck. " 'Rico . . like . . beeg beds . . like beeg . . sheeps!" he said. She hugged him and thought again she could not bear to send him back to Italy not knowing what would happen to him in the future.

She chose one of her prettiest evening-gowns for dinner. She told herself as she did so that it was unlikely that the Duke would notice what she was wearing. But at least it would be in keeping with the luxury and beauty of the house. Everywhere she looked she saw treasures which delighted her. She wished that her father and mother could see them too.

When she went downstairs it was to find the Duke alone in the drawing-room. He was looking very smart and extremely impressive in his evening clothes. He smiled at her as she came across the room towards him and said: "Although it would seem very reprehensible to my Aunt Anne, we are dining alone."

Luella's heart gave a leap for joy as he went on: "My secretary's wife is unfortunately away, but he had arranged for his sister-in-law, who is older and married to the son of a bishop, to come and be your chaperon." The way he said it made it sound so funny that Luella laughed. "I am sure she will prove very effective," the Duke said, "but as she has to attend a church meeting, she cannot join us until after dinner."

"I am sure your Aunt will be delighted that I am to be so well looked after," Luella said demurely. They drank a glass of champagne before dinner was announced.

Luella found herself in a most attractive dining-room. It was painted in the pale green which she knew was a favourite colour of Robert Adam. In the alcoves there were statues of Greek gods skilfully lit from behind. "This is the loveliest room I have ever seen!" Luella said to the Duke.

"That is what I thought myself when I first came here," the Duke said, "and I am very fortunate in knowing it is now mine."

The way he spoke made Luella know that it meant a great deal to him. It also made her aware once again of his importance. She could understand how his Aunt, as well as his other relatives, wanted him to marry somebody whose blood was as 'blue' as his.

"I must enjoy his company while I can," she told herself, "for once all this is settled, I suppose I shall never see him again." It hurt her to know that he would pass out of her life with the same speed that he had come into it.

As they were being served the Duke said: "I have been thinking. It is strange that your father, considering how well he wrote, has published only one book."

"He started to write when he was young," Luella answered, "having left Oxford with a first class degree in History." She saw the Duke was interested and went on: "He wrote articles for the Royal Geographical Society, using a number of different names. It was only recently that he started using his own."

She thought the Duke was going to ask the reason for that and said quickly: "The Royal Geographical Society were delighted with the articles he wrote about different parts of the world. They not only paid him well, but also kept begging him for more."

The Duke gave an exclamation. "Surely you realise what that means?"

"What does it mean?" Luella enquired.

"It means that you have at least two further books to go to the publishers."

Luella stared at him. "I never . . thought of . . that!"

"I have read articles in the Geographical Magazine," the Duke said, "and I can imagine nothing more attractive to the public than if your father's articles were put together, given a good title and published as a book."

Luella clasped her hands together. "That is clever of you!" she exclaimed. "It was . . stupid of me not to . . think of it."

"You have the articles?" the Duke enquired.

"Yes, I packed Papa's new book with everything else he wrote and brought them back from Italy. They are in a box upstairs."

"I think your father's publishers," the Duke said, "will be delighted when they hear what you have to show them."

"I cannot imagine why I never thought of the articles being put together into a book. But they are fascinating and I know people will enjoy them."

"I am sure it would be a best-seller," the Duke agreed. "A lot of people find it hard to get through a whole volume, but they would enjoy a book that is almost like a collection of short stories, which, of course, is exactly what they are."

"I can only say .. thank you, thank you .. once again," Luella said. She thought if the publishers agreed it would certainly make it possible for her to have Enrico with her.

Then she knew that it might still be expensive. She wondered whether she could beg the Duke for a small cottage on his estate.

As if he read her thoughts, he said: "I must advise you once again, Luella, not to be too determined to look after Enrico. As I have already said, you are very young, and an adopted child might make things more difficult for you than they are already."

"It will be difficult," Luella agreed in a small voice, "if I have to .. ask Papa's relatives not only to have me, but Enrico as well." She sighed and then went on: "But perhaps I can find somewhere cheap where we could live and where there would be a school nearby in which he could be educated."

The Duke did not answer. She thought perhaps he was angry that she did not immediately say she would give up her idea of looking after Enrico.

Fortunately, after they were served with the next course, he started to talk of something else. She then encouraged him to tell her the history of some of the treasures that were in this house as well as those in the Castle.

"I am only just learning about them myself," the Duke admitted.

"It must be very exciting," Luella remarked, "like having an Aladdin's cave all to yourself."

The Duke smiled. "Now you are making me feel greedy, or else, like my relatives, you are trying to push me into matrimony."

Luella remembered what the Dowager Marchioness had said. She thought that if the Queen insisted on finding him a bride, it would be impossible for him to refuse whatever suggestion she might make.

She did not say anything and the Duke went on: "I know you are thinking of Enrico, but you have to remember that one day you will marry and have children of your own." He stopped for a moment and smiled at her. "Your husband may resent having an Italian boy attached to his family, whether he likes it or not."

Luella did not answer and after a moment he said: "I have had a message to say that the Ambassador will call on me at three o'clock tomorrow afternoon. So I suggest we do not make any plans about Enrico, nor shall I see my solicitors until after I have talked to him."

"I am praying that he will be .. able to do .. something for you," Luella said softly.

"That is what I am hoping," the Duke replied. "At the same time, he may not wish to become involved in anything so unpleasant."

Luella wanted to protest that no Italian who was decent would allow Signor Vecchio to behave in such an appalling manner. Then she thought to say so would only spoil the evening. It was, as the Duke had said, impossible for them to come to any conclusion until after putting the case to the Ambassador.

She therefore talked about pictures. She discovered that, in fact, the Duke knew a great deal about them. Although he had not visited as many countries as she had, they compared notes on quite a number of pictures they both admired. They sat at the dining-room table for a long time before they went into the drawing-room.

They had only just sat down to continue their conversation when the door opened. "Mrs Alcombe, Your Grace," the butler announced.

As she came into the room, Luella could not help thinking Mrs Alcombe looked exactly as a Christian worker would look.

"You must forgive me, Your Grace, for not coming sooner," she said to the Duke, holding out her hand, "but there was a meeting I was obliged to attend. It was about the propagation of the Gospel in the Far East."

"I am very grateful to you, Mrs Alcombe, for coming at such short notice," the Duke replied. "I can only express my regret at the inconvenience."

"It is always a pleasure to come here, Your Grace," Mrs Alcombe answered.

"Now let me introduce you to the young lady you are chaperoning," the Duke said. "Miss Luella Hanley, whose father was a distinguished author."

"So my brother-in-law told me," Mrs Alcombe said, "but I am afraid I have not read any of his books, as I have so much to read for the Church." She paused, and as no one said anything, she went on: "We are collecting a library of books that are suitable to send abroad to any missionary who requires them for his congregation."

"I have no doubt that will be a difficult task," the Duke remarked, "as of course most natives cannot read even their own language."

"That is so," Mrs Alcombe sighed. "Nevertheless, we must do our best to civilise the poor souls. And of course, a great number of them also require clothing."

Luella could not help being aware that the Duke's eyes were twinkling. But he said in a quite serious voice: "I feel sure no one can help these poor people better than you, Mrs Alcombe."

"That's what I like to think, Your Grace."

Because Luella was certain the conversation was boring the Duke, she rose and said she wanted to go to bed. Mrs Alcombe agreed. They said goodnight to the Duke and went up the stairs together. Luella found a maid who showed Mrs Alcombe to the room in which she was to sleep. Then she went to her own.

As she did so she thought how glad she was that Mrs Alcombe had been late in coming and had not been with her and the Duke at dinner. "I want to go on talking to him," she told herself. She realised the Duke was still downstairs and it would be an easy matter to slip back and be with him.

Even as she thought of it, she was shocked at the idea. And yet, all the time she was undressing she was thinking that she might be with him. She could be listening to his deep voice, and watching for the twinkle in his eyes when something amused him. "Perhaps after tomorrow when the Ambassador has been, I will never see him again," she told herself as she got into bed. It was then she realised how much this would hurt her.

In the short time she had known him, the Duke had somehow occupied her thoughts to the exclusion of everything else. Suddenly she realised the danger of it. If the Duke was to haunt her, how could she find any other man attractive? How would it be possible for her to go on thinking about him, when she did not see him? She knew she would feel even more lonely than she had when her father had died. The questions seemed to crowd in on her, impressing themselves on her mind until she could not sleep.

Finally she got out of bed and went to the window to pull back the curtains. The stars filled the sky as they had last night as she peeped out of her window in the Castle. Now as she looked up at them she realised she was reaching for the stars. It was, in fact, the most foolish thing she had done in her whole life. "How could I be so idiotic as to fall in love with a man who is as far away from me as the stars?" she asked herself. "A man to whom I can never mean anything."

She felt the tears come into her eyes. Because it was impossible to see the stars clearly, she closed the curtains. Luella got back into bed and cried as she had not cried since her father's funeral. She was honest enough with herself to know that she was not crying now for her father, but for a star that was completely out of reach.

The next morning Luella was not called very early. By the time she had dressed Enrico she found when she went downstairs that the Duke had already had his breakfast, and was in the study with his secretary.

There was a large choice of dishes. Hewitt, the butler, told them that as His Grace was going to be busy all morning, he had suggested they might like to go driving in the park. Enrico grew excited at the idea of seeing the big horses again.

An open victoria was brought round to the front door. Luella and he set off in style. They drove down Rotten Row. She saw smart gentlemen on horseback talking to beautiful ladies in open carriages like their own. "They belong to the Duke's world," she thought, "and I am not a part of it."

Enrico was thrilled by everything he saw. He jumped up and down pointing out to Luella first one horse, then another. When he saw some children on horseback who were about the same age as himself, he demanded that he too should be allowed to ride. Luella thought that if he lived with her she would somehow have to contrive to afford a pony, even if it was only a very cheap one.

Once again the difficulties of her future were sweeping over her. She was afraid that, because he disapproved, the Duke would not be anxious to rent her a cottage on his estate. She had no idea at the moment who else she could ask. "This afternoon," she decided, "I must ask him if his secretary would be kind enough to try to find any of Papa's relations who might help me."

She was hoping that the Duke had not forgotten to arrange for her father's publishers to come to the house. That was more important than anything else.

When they returned to Park Lane it was time for luncheon. Luella, as she washed her hands, thought with a leap of her heart that she would see the Duke. She was, however, disappointed when she came downstairs to find that, not only was Mrs Alcombe having luncheon with them, there were also three friends of the Duke who had turned up unexpectedly.

They were, she discovered, neighbours from the country. They were joining with him in constructing a race-course in the local vicinity. It would create employment for the local men. It would also be a place where they could try out their racehorses before they entered them at Newmarket or the other established race-courses. The three men and the Duke had a lot to discuss.

Luella could only listen and think as she watched him how handsome he was. He was also, she realised, extremely intelligent, and in some way remarkably like her father. He always seemed to have something original to suggest which had not occurred to other people. As she watched him she knew it was a joy and a delight she did not like to express even to herself.

Enrico ate a large meal after which Luella took him into another room on the ground floor. She knew it was where the Duke would entertain the Italian Ambassador when he arrived. Enrico, however, wanted to play with the toys that had been found for him upstairs. She took him up to the boudoir which opened out of his bedroom and told the housemaid who had looked after him to keep him amused.

"He be ever so 'appy with them toys, Miss," the housemaid said, "and I've brought some more down from t'attics. There's a great big pile of 'em up there, an' it seems a pity to waste 'em."

"It does indeed," Luella agreed, "and thank you very much for thinking of it."

Enrico was delighted with his new toys. He started to set them out around him on the floor and Luella returned downstairs. As she did so she saw that the three men who had come to luncheon were departing.

Now, she thought, she could be alone with the Duke. Mrs Alcombe had said earlier that she had a meeting this afternoon and would not be back until tea time. Luella went to the room where the Ambassador was to be entertained and waited.

The Duke, having said goodbye to his friends, came in smiling. "I thought I might find you here, Luella," he said. "Where is the boy?"

"He is upstairs playing with some more toys which have been found in the attic," Luella replied.

"That is yet another place I have to examine,"

the Duke observed. "Apart from toys for Enrico, there may be other things there for me to add to my Aladdin's cave."

"It must be very exciting for you," Luella smiled.

"It is indeed," the Duke agreed. "Like your father I, too, enjoy discovering new lands and new peoples."

Luella thought that was what he would be doing when she was no longer with him. She was just about to ask him where he was going when the door opened and Hewitt announced: "His Excellency the Italian Ambassador."

A man came into the room who was quite obviously Italian – not very tall, but good-looking. Luella thought there was something vaguely familiar about his face. Then she told herself that one Italian was very much like another.

The Ambassador was certainly a distinguished man. The Duke greeted him profusely. "It is most kind of you to come to visit me at such short notice, Your Excellency."

"You told me the matter was urgent," the Ambassador replied, speaking good English. "I therefore came as quickly as I could."

"I am extremely grateful to you," the Duke said. "May I offer you some refreshment?"

The Ambassador shook his head. "Thank you, but I have just come from a large and rather boring luncheon."

The Duke smiled and indicated a chair near the fireplace. He hesitated before he said to Luella: "I think, Miss Hanley, I should speak to His Excellency alone. I will send a servant to tell you when I would like you to bring the little boy downstairs to meet him."

"Y.yes . . of course," Luella replied. She thought a little guiltily she should have suggested this herself. She went quickly from the room, closing the door behind her. As she walked up the stairs she was thinking that of course the Duke would have been embarrassed to talk about Tia in front of her. That was why he had sent her away.

Enrico was still entranced by his toys. He was pushing a wooden train under some of the chairs and making a noise like a railway engine.

Watching Enrico, his eyes bright and excited, Luella thought that, whatever the Duke might say, she would not let him back to the sordid house from which he had come. Nor would she allow him to be at the mercy of Signor Vecchio. "He is cruel and wicked," she told herself, "and even if I have to scrub floors, I will keep Enrico away from a man like that!"

It seemed to her a long time before finally a footman came to the door to say: "His Grace would be obliged if Miss Hanley an' the young gentleman would join him downstairs."

"Come along, Enrico," Luella said. "The Duke wants to see us, and there is a gentleman with him who is Italian, like you."

"I want to play with my trains," Enrico grumbled in his own language.

"They will be here when you come back," Luella said.

Enrico, however, protested. Finally a compromise was reached when Luella said he could bring the engine with him. Carrying it in his arms, he followed Luella down the stairs.

As they drew near to the door of the sitting-room she said: "Remember to bow to the Italian gentleman, and call him 'Your Excellency'."

"Why?" Enrico enquired.

"Because he is a very important man."

Enrico considered this for a moment. Then he said: " 'Rico . . show . . his fast . . train."

"I am sure he will appreciate that," Luella smiled, "but do not forget to say 'Your Excellency'."

She repeated it in Italian and thought that Enrico understood.

A footman who had been waiting in the corridor announced them. They went in hand-in-hand to find the Duke standing with his back to the fireplace. The Ambassador was sitting comfortably in an armchair.

When Luella came towards them he rose to his feet, and the Duke said: "Your Excellency, allow me to introduce Miss Hanley, who has, as I told you, been extremely helpful to me."

The Ambassador smiled and held out his hand to Luella who said: "It is an honour to meet Your Excellency."

"His Grace has been telling me about your father," the Ambassador replied, "and I will be extremely interested to read his new book, especially what he has to say about St. Peter's and of course the Cathedral in Milan."

"I am hoping to get it published quite soon," Luella replied.

"Now let me look at this young man about whom

I have been told so much," the Ambassador said. He bent towards Enrico who was holding his engine tightly as if he was afraid it might be taken away from him. "I am told your name is Enrico," the Ambassador said in Italian.

As the little boy glanced up at him, Luella saw the Ambassador stiffen. He was staring at the child in a strange manner. Because she felt frightened for Enrico, she asked quickly: "What .. is it? What is .. wrong?"

The Ambassador did not answer. He was just looking down at Enrico with an incredulous expression on his face. Finally he said in a voice that sounded very different from the way it had before: "When did you say this child was born?"

"If Vecchio is to be believed," the Duke replied, "on February 2nd, 1875."

The Ambassador was silent, still staring at Enrico, and the Duke asked: "Why do you ask? Is something wrong?"

The Ambassador straightened himself. As he did so Luella looked at him questioningly. She was then aware why she had thought there was something familiar about him. His eyebrows turned up at the sides and, although it was not very marked, there was definitely a widow's peak in the centre of his forehead. She gave a little gasp and the Ambassador said slowly in English: "I believe this boy to be my son!"

"Yours?" the Duke exclaimed in astonishment. Then as he looked at the Ambassador in the same way that Luella was doing, he, too, recognised the similarities between them.

The Ambassador sat down heavily in a chair as if his legs could no longer support him.

Enrico put his engine down on the floor. He began to push it under the chairs as if they were railway tunnels.

For a moment no one spoke.

At last the Ambassador said: "Your Grace told me the dates when you were in Milan. I was there just a fortnight before you." The two men looked at each other and there was no need to say any more. Luella realised that the Ambassador must have been attracted to Tia in the same way that the Duke had been.

"There is certainly a distinct resemblance," the Duke said slowly.

"The way our eyebrows are shaped is something that runs in the family," the Ambassador said, "and many of my relations, as well as myself, have what you call a 'widow's peak' in the centre of the forehead."

"Both those features are very obvious in Enrico," the Duke remarked.

"As they have never been known in any other family, except ours," the Ambassador finished.

"Then . . what are you . . going to . . do . . about it?" Luella asked in a frightened voice.

The Ambassador turned to smile at her before he said: "Miss Hanley, you have brought me the son I have always longed for, but thought was impossible for me to have."

Before Luella or the Duke could speak he went on: "My first wife who died ten years ago left me with two daughters. It will be five years next month since I married again and, to be frank, hoped to have a son. Then, unfortunately, my wife was involved in a carriage accident and though she has completely recovered from it, the doctors have said it is impossible for her to bear a child." There was a note in His Excellency's voice which told Luella what a blow that had been to him.

He then continued: "We have been talking of adopting a boy since, as you doubtless know, Italian women never feel complete without a family around them."

"Y.you do not . . think," Luella said hesitatingly, "that your wife will . . resent Enrico . . actually being . . your own . . s.son?"

"It happened before I had even met my wife," the Ambassador replied. "I was a lonely widower and I know she will understand."

"Oh . . I am glad . . so very glad!" Luella exclaimed. "Enrico is such a . . dear little boy . . and has beautiful manners . . which makes it obvious he has been very well brought up."

The Ambassador glanced at the Duke and said: "That is what we might have expected of Tia, who herself was the illegitimate daughter of an aristocrat. At the same time, this child must have nothing whatsoever to do with Vecchio!'

"That is . . exactly what we have been . . thinking," Luella said. "How could we send him . . back to that . . wicked man or to the sordid house in which he was living."

The Ambassador looked surprised. "Tia had a

very pleasant flat," he answered, speaking as if to himself.

"I expect as soon as she died another of Vecchio's protégées took it over," the Duke said sarcastically.

"And the child would have been sent to live with the servants," the Ambassador finished.

"I was so . . frightened," Luella interposed, "that he would have to return . . there."

"You need no longer worry about him," the Ambassador assured her. "As I have already told His Grace, Vecchio will be dealt with immediately, so that this sort of thing can never happen again."

Luella's eyes widened. "How . . will you . . prevent it?" she asked.

"Quite easily," the Ambassador replied. "We have, in Milan, known of his activities for a long time, but he was always clever enough to leave no evidence, and always covered his tracks."

"What you are saying is that . . now you have the . . letter and the . . fraudulent marriage certificate!" Luella exclaimed.

"I have those," His Excellency said, "and I also have the evidence which His Grace has given me."

"Then . . you do not . . need mine?" Luella enquired.

The Ambassador shook his head. "His Grace is anxious that you should not be brought into this unsavoury affair, and I agree with him. In fact, to save the good name of Milan, the case against Vecchio will be held in private. Nothing will be allowed to get into the press."

He paused before he went on: "I am, however, convinced that long before the case comes to trial Vecchio will disappear, perhaps to the East, or to Africa, and we shall never be troubled by him again."

"Oh .. I hope .. that is what .. happens!" Luella cried.

"It will, my dear young lady, I am almost certain of it!" the Ambassador said. He smiled at Luella, then looked towards the Duke. "I am sure you will understand, Your Grace," he said, "that I want to take my son home with me now."

"But of course," the Duke agreed. "Yours is obviously the higher claim."

The Ambassador laughed. "I want to see my wife's face when I give her a replica of myself." He walked across the room to where Enrico was still busy with his train. He put out his hand and said in Italian: "Will you come with me, Enrico? I will give you a bigger train than that, and it will go by itself when you wind it up."

"A bigger train?" Enrico repeated. " 'Rico would like that."

"Come along then," the Ambassador said. "We will buy it on our way home."

"Buy it now?" Enrico enquired as if to make certain he had heard aright.

"We will go to the shop in my carriage," the Ambassador promised.

Enrico gave a little skip for joy. Taking him by the hand, the Ambassador started to lead him towards the door. Enrico bent down to pick up his engine. " 'Rico bring this one too," the little boy said.

The Ambassador laughed. "There speaks a true Italian," he said to the Duke, "who is cute enough never to miss an opportunity!"

The Duke laughed too. Then the Ambassador, who seemed to have become younger as if touched by a magic wand, said: "I will deal with everything, Your Grace, and thank you, Miss Hanley, from the bottom of my heart for bringing me what I have always wanted more than anything else in the world!"

Before the Duke or Luella could speak he was gone. They could hear Enrico chattering excitedly as they went down the corridor. The Ambassador was answering him, also with a note of excitement in his voice.

Luella looked at the empty doorway, then at the Duke. Quite unexpectedly he laughed. "No farewells," he said, "no thanks! Just the promise of a bigger train and a new home!"

"He is a dear little boy, and I shall miss him," Luella said ruefully.

"The Enricos of this world always fall on their feet," the Duke remarked, "and now all our difficulties are solved."

"*Yours* are," Luella said, "and I am very, very glad."

"As you just said – mine are," the Duke said. "Now I have to think about yours."

"I . . I do not want to be a . . trouble to you now it is . . all over," Luella murmured.

"But you *do* trouble me, Luella," the Duke insisted. "You trouble me very much!" He spoke quietly and she looked at him, in surprise. Then he said: "I hope *you* do not intend to walk away from me, because that is something I shall certainly prevent!"

Chapter Seven

Luella looked at the Duke with wide eyes. Then he moved a little nearer to her. Because she was nervous she said: "I . . I do not . . understand."

"Then let me explain," the Duke said. As he spoke he put his arms around her, holding her close, then his lips came down on hers.

For a moment Luella felt she must be dreaming and it could not be true. A feeling of ecstasy shot through her. As the Duke kissed her and went on kissing her she knew that he felt the same. He kissed her until the room seemed to whirl round them.

Then the door started to open and he took his arms from her, so quickly that she almost fell. The back of a chair saved her and she felt her breath coming quickly from between her lips. She was finding it hard to believe that her feet were still on the ground.

Hewitt crossed the room to the Duke. "A letter's just arrived for Your Grace from Windsor Castle."

He held the letter out on a silver salver, but the Duke waved it away. "Put it on my desk," he said.

Hewitt did as he was told, and at that moment Mrs Alcombe came bustling into the room. "I am so sorry, Your Grace, to be late," she said, "but we had a most tempestuous meeting with everybody arguing. I thought it would never end!"

The Duke did not reply and she went up to Luella and said: "I was so sorry, my dear, not to see you this morning before I left. I really have had a most exhausting day, but with one or two satisfactory results, which I must tell you about."

It seemed to Luella as if her voice came from a very long distance as she replied: "Thank you, but now I have to go upstairs."

She walked from the room without looking at the Duke. Only when she was outside in the corridor did she start to run. She ran through the hall, up the stairs and into her bedroom. Once there, she shut the door and sitting down in a chair covered her face with her hands. Her whole body seemed to be pulsating with the wonder of the Duke's kisses.

At the same time, the letter had come from Windsor Castle. She knew it was the death-knell to her happiness. She was quite sure that it contained, as the Dowager Marchioness had hinted, a command from the Queen for the Duke to go to the Castle. There, she thought, he would be told whom he was expected to marry.

"I love him .. I love him!" she told herself in a broken whisper. Once again in her mind she was looking at the stars, knowing they were out of reach.

Because she was afraid that Mrs Alcombe might follow her to find out if anything was wrong, she lay down on the bed. She shut her eyes. If anybody did come in they would think she was asleep and would not disturb her. All she wanted to do was to think about the Duke and her love for him, hopeless though it might be. There was, however, no sign of Mrs Alcombe.

It was nearly two hours later that a maid came into the room. "I'll get your bath ready, Miss," she said.

"Thank you," Luella answered. When she had finished her bath she decided that she could not go downstairs and face the Duke. It would be an agony to have to talk politely in front of Mrs Alcombe.

It would be an even greater agony later when he told her what the letter from Windsor Castle contained. Luella knew suddenly that she could not bear to hear him say in actual words that their love was hopeless. "He may think he loves me now," she thought, "but he will soon forget me, although I will never . . never forget him."

The maid was asking her what she would like to wear. "I have a headache," Luella replied. "Would you be kind enough to tell His Grace that I am obliged to stay in bed?"

"Oh, I'm sorry, Miss," the maid said, "but I 'spect yer'd like some warm soup an' somethin' else t'eat?"

"That would be very kind," Luella said, "and my head is really aching." She knew the actual truth was that it was her heart that was aching. It was aching with an agony that was inexpressible. It seemed to make the whole world dark and without a glimmer of hope.

She was in bed when Mrs Alcombe came into the room. "I am so sorry to hear you have a headache," she said, "I hope it's not the beginning of a cold."

"I .. I am sure I will be .. all right by tomorrow," Luella replied, "but my mother always said that if one had a headache, the best thing to do was to .. sleep it .. off."

"Now that's strange," Mrs Alcombe said, "for my mother always said the same thing, and it's what I've always adhered to myself. And goodness knows, I've had enough headaches with all these meetings to organise and so much to do for those poor primitive people in Africa."

"I am .. sure they are .. very grateful," Luella murmured.

Mrs Alcombe went into a long explanation as to why very few people appreciated what was being done for them. Especially, she added, if it concerned the soul rather than the body. When she finally left the room, Luella thought how bored the Duke would be if she talked to him like that all through dinner.

But she knew the one thing she could not do was to sit watching him. "If only we could be alone again," she thought. She longed for him with an agony that made her cry out from the pain of it.

It was only after she had eaten a little and the tray had been removed that she knew what she had to do. The Duke was downstairs, but she could not go to him. And if she did, what could she say? "I must go away," she decided, "and the quicker the better!"

When the maid came in and asked if there was anything else she required she said: "Please tell Mrs Alcombe I am going to sleep and do not wish to be disturbed."

" 'Course I will, Miss," the maid said, "an' I knows she's sorry, as we all are, that you're feelin' poorly."

"Thank you," Luella said. "You are very kind."

The maid left the room leaving only an oil-lamp burning on a table beside the bed. When Luella was certain she would not return, she got out of bed. Opening out of her bedroom was a large cupboard. There she found the small case that had contained Enrico's clothes. She thought she could easily carry it herself.

She placed some of her clothes in it and took the manuscript of her father's book out of the box which had not been unpacked since she arrived. Some of the articles he had written she also put in the small suitcase; enough to make the book the Duke had suggested. "I will call on Papa's publishers," she thought. "I must swear them to secrecy, in case the Duke should try to find me." She thought with a little sigh that was unlikely.

She told herself that if the publishers were interested in her father's book and articles, they would find her somewhere cheap to stay. Then she could discover, as she had meant to do when she came to England, where her father's relatives lived. "I am sure his publishers will help me," she thought.

By the time she had packed the case she heard footsteps outside in the corridor. She guessed it was Mrs Alcombe on her way to bed. If the Duke had not yet come up to his room, he was likely to be in the study. He would doubtless be thinking out how to answer the Queen's command.

"If I went to him now we would be . . alone and he would . . kiss me again," Luella could not help thinking. The idea sent a shaft of fire streaking through her body. It brought back for an instant the ecstasy she had known when he kissed her before. Then she knew that the one thing she could never do if she really loved him was to hurt him in any way. "I . . love him! I love . . him!" The words kept repeating themselves over and over in her mind as she dressed.

She put on the pretty gown with the coat she had worn on the journey to London. When she was ready she very cautiously opened her bedroom door. Lights were still burning in some of the silver sconces in the corridor. She could therefore see to the end of the passage where the stairs joined it. The big chandelier in the hall was no longer alight.

She had already worked out how she could leave the house. There would be a night footman on duty near the front who would think it strange for her to be going out alone at night. He might try to dissuade her.

Then she remembered how Enrico had told her about a door in the wall at the end of the garden which led into the mews. She thought he had probably obtained the information from a maid. He had taken Luella to the window and pointing across the garden said: " 'Rico ride . . beeg . . horses. They in . . stables . . there."

"We will go and see them as soon as we have time," Luella had promised.

"Go .. now! Go .. now!" he had demanded.

As it was time for them to go downstairs, she had told him they would have to wait until tomorrow morning. How could she have guessed then that by tomorrow morning Enrico would have gone to a happy home? She, on the other hand, would be completely alone in the world with only her memories of the Duke.

She slipped out through her bedroom door and walked on tip-toe down the corridor. She knew that the staircase at the far end of it was used only by the servants. Her suitcase was not heavy, only cumbersome. She manoeuvred it carefully down the stairs so as not to make a noise. She had no difficulty in finding the door that led into the garden. It was not bolted and she opened it easily.

It was a warm night without a wind. The moon and the stars were turning the leaves to silver. The trunks of the large trees created deep shadows over the well-kept lawn.

Carrying her suitcase in her right hand, Luella started to walk on the grass, so that her feet would make no sound. She had nearly reached the wall in which was the door leading into the mews. Suddenly she was aware of a movement. Then a man appeared in front of her. Because she was so startled she gave a little scream. As she put her hand to her mouth to suppress it, she realised it was the Duke.

"Whatever are you doing out here at this time of the night?" he asked. "And where on earth are you going?"

"D.Do not .. stop me . . .." Luella begged. "I .. I have to .. go away!"

"Go away? But why?"

She wanted to explain, but suddenly it was impossible for her to speak. She could only try to control the tears that threatened to pour down her cheeks.

Gently he took the suitcase from her and putting his arm around her he said: "I have been sitting here thinking about you. Now, come and sit down and tell me what all this is about."

Luella saw a wooden seat under the trees as he drew her towards it. She sat down, pulling her hat from her head, and put her hand to her forehead.

"You said you had a headache," the Duke remarked quietly, "but I thought you were just being wise and avoiding the voluble Mrs Alcombe! How could you be so unkind as to run away from me?"

"I .. I have to .. go!" Luella stammered.

"But why? Why?"

The Duke obviously demanded an answer, and after what seemed a long pause Luella said: "Y.you .. have to be .. married to somebody whom .. the Queen has .. chosen for you."

"So that is why you are leaving me!" the Duke exclaimed. "My darling, do you really think I could marry anyone but you?" His voice deepened as he spoke and he put his arms round her. Before she could prevent it, his lips held hers captive. He kissed her possessively and passionately, as if he was afraid she might have left him.

Only when they were both breathless did he raise his head to say: "Now tell me you love me!"

"I . . I love you! I . . love you!" Luella said. "But . . because I . . love you . . I cannot . . hurt you."

"You could hurt me only if you left me," the Duke said. "I have never before been in love as I love you, my precious, and if I lost you I would not wish to go on living."

"You must . . not say that . . you must . . not!" Luella cried. "And . . even if you do not . . obey the Queen . . you cannot . . m.marry me."

She could see the Duke in the moonlight staring at her in astonishment before he asked: "What are you saying?"

"It would . . hurt you in your . . position if you . . married me."

"That is absolute nonsense!" the Duke said. "Your father was respected as a writer, and we will make him even better known. And anyone who sees you, my beautiful one, will understand why I wanted to marry you."

"It is . . not only that," Luella whispered, "you . . must not . . marry me . . it is impossible for you to do so."

The Duke pulled her closer to him. "I may be very stupid," he said, "but you will have to explain to me why you feel like this."

"Papa always said . . that I was to . . tell no one," Luella replied. "But he thought that if I . . married someone . . ordinary . . it would . . not matter." She gave a little sob before she went on: "But . . but you are . . not ordinary . . you are *extra*ordinary . . and very important . . and I . . I could not . . spoil your l.life."

The Duke's arms tightened. "I do not understand, my lovely one. Tell me what this is all about. I am becoming more and more bewildered, but at the same time, more and more sure that you are the only person in the whole world who can make me happy."

As if he could not help himself, he turned her face up to his and kissed her again. This time his kisses were fierce and demanding. She felt as if she melted into him and was a part of him. They were no longer two people, but one. She knew her heart was beating frantically, and the Duke's was too. She thought nothing could be more perfect than their love. As she had longed to do, she was touching the stars.

Then as the Duke raised his head, she came down to earth. "Now tell me my darling one, whatever it is, and we can face it together."

Luella turned her face against him. Because she knew she had to tell him what he wanted to know she said in a small voice: "I . . I told you that Papa . . after he left Oxford . . wrote articles for the . . Royal Geographical Society. He was twenty-four years old, when they asked him to do a special one about . . Windsor Castle."

She paused as she felt the Duke kiss her hair and it sent a little thrill through her. With an effort she forced herself to go on: "It was when he was there . . and Queen Victoria gave him permission to . . stay in the Castle . . that he met by chance . . one of Her Majesty's guests."

Luella was aware that the Duke was now listening intently as she continued: "The Queen had . . sent for Princess Stephanie of Sweden to come to England because she .. wished her to marry one of Prince Albert's relations .. a member of .. the Saxe-Coburg family."

"I think I can guess where this story is leading!" the Duke exclaimed.

"They met .. two or three times .. and .. fell in love with each other."

"Go on," the Duke said with his lips against her forehead.

"Because they .. knew that the .. Queen would .. never for .. one minute consider .. allowing Princess Stephanie to .. marry Papa .. they decided what they .. must .. do."

"They eloped!" the Duke exclaimed.

"Y.yes .. they ran away in the middle of the night and went to Tilbury .. There they boarded the first .. ship that was .. due to put to .. sea .. and once they were .. out in the ocean .. they asked .. the Captain to .. marry them."

"I think that was very romantic," the Duke said.

"The ship they boarded .. happened to be going to India," Luella went on. "That was in the days before the .. Suez Canal was opened .. and it took them weeks and weeks to get there." Her voice was very soft and she continued: "Mama always said it was like .. being in Heaven being .. alone with Papa .. and knowing that .. no one could .. find them .. or reproach them for .. what they had done."

"They were not found?" the Duke asked.

"No, not then," Luella answered. "When they reached India they moved from place to place, going up to the Himalayas and into Nepal."

"They could afford so much travelling?" the Duke asked.

"Papa had been left some money by his godfather, besides an allowance his father made him, and wherever they stayed he sent an article under a different name to the Royal Geographical Society."

"So that is why you lived abroad," the Duke remarked.

"I was born after they had been married for four years," Luella said, "and I went with them everywhere. But Papa had learned that the King of Sweden was furious, and Mama's father, who was a cousin of the King, ordered that her name was never to be mentioned again." She sighed before she added: "We always . . supposed that Queen Victoria was no less . . annoyed."

"I think it was very sensible of your father to do what he did," the Duke said.

"They were so very . . very happy," Luella whispered. "At the . . same time, Papa was not a . . D.Duke. And as a Duke . . you have a responsibility to look after . . your relatives . . and also your . . estates . . and your position is . . very . . very important . . not only to you . . but to so many other p.people."

"And what about you?" the Duke asked.

"I . . love you . . you know I love you," Luella said unhappily, "but I love you . . too much to do . . anything that would . . spoil your l.life." The last words were incoherent because the tears were running down her face.

The Duke took a handkerchief from a pocket and gently wiped them away. At the same time he was holding her very close. Then he said: "This has been too much for you, my precious one. I am going to take you back inside the house, and I want you to go to bed. We will talk again about everything in the morning."

"It would be . . better if you . . let me go away . . n.now," Luella murmured.

"Do you think I would allow you to go anywhere alone?" the Duke asked. "If you love me, I love you, and I must protect you, take care of you, and never allow you to go into danger." He spoke so firmly that Luella knew there would be no point in arguing with him.

He got up from the wooden seat, took her hands in his and raised her to her feet. Putting one arm round her, he picked up her case in his other hand. They walked together over the grass and went into the house by the garden door. They did not speak.

The Duke led her up the side-staircase as if he knew instinctively that was the way she had left. When they reached her bedroom door he opened it to see that the oil-lamp was still burning beside her bed. He looked at her for a long moment before he said: "I want you to promise me, my darling, on everything you hold sacred that you will not run away during the night, but will be here in the morning."

There was a touch of laughter in his voice as he went on: "If you do not promise me, then of course I shall have to stay with you all night, and I am sure Mrs Alcombe will be deeply shocked!"

Because his eyes were twinkling, Luella could not help giving a little chuckle. "I give you . . my word," she said. "I will be . . here in . . the morning . . but, darling, darling . . you know we have to . . leave each other . . though every time I . . see you and you . . kiss me . . I love you . . more and more."

"That is exactly what I want you to do," the Duke said. He pulled her close and kissed her until once again it was impossible to think of anything but him. An ecstasy was rising within her until she felt as if she was utterly consumed by it.

Then, so suddenly that she almost fell, the Duke released her. He strode out of the room and shut the door behind him.

She was alone. Yet she felt as if her whole body was pulsating with the wonder and glory he had given her. She was no longer a human being, but one with the stars. "I . . love him . . Oh . . God . . I love him! How can I . . leave him?" she asked.

Because she felt she had to obey the Duke she got into bed. The tears were trickling down her cheeks, but after a while she fell asleep.

Luella awoke and thought it must be later than she was usually called. She looked at the clock and, thinking something must be wrong, she rang the bell.

A maid came in and started to draw back the curtains. "G'mornin', Miss," she said. "His Grace said as I wasn't t'call you. But he'd be grateful if you'd come downstairs at twelve o'clock."

"At twelve o'clock?" Luella repeated, "but . . what is the time now?"

"It's nearly eleven, Miss."

"I thought the clock must be wrong!" Luella exclaimed.

"You've got an hour to get ready, Miss," the maid said soothingly, "an' His Grace asked I to tell you you're goin' t'the country."

Luella felt her heart leap. At the same time her conscience was telling her that she ought not to go. It would make things even worse to have to say goodbye in the Castle.

And yet she had a feeling that he wanted to show her something there before they said goodbye. That too would be an agony. Because she was afraid of crying, she tried not to think of the Duke as she dressed.

The maid packed her clothes into the same trunk in which they had come to London. It was only when she was taking the things out of the small case she had packed last night that Luella realised her father's book and the magazine articles were not there.

As she stared at the half-empty case in surprise, the maid said: "I forgets t' tell you, Miss. His Grace wanted th' book an' th' papers, so I crept in ever so quiet-like while you was still asleep an' got 'em. Was that right?"

"Yes, of course, it was quite all right," Luella answered. She thought it was so like the Duke to have remembered that she wanted her father's publishers to have the manuscript of his book. "I am sure," she thought, "he will arrange for them to give me enough money to keep myself on."

At the same time she suspected he would insist upon her seeking out her relations. It would certainly be better if she had some money of her own and was not dependent on them. She had no wish to live with anybody, she thought, except of course, him. "I . . love . . him," she said beneath her breath. Once again the pain was back in her heart.

It was two minutes to twelve when Luella looked at herself in the mirror. She realised that without thinking about it she had put on her prettiest gown. It had a small bolero to wear over it. The hat which matched it was trimmed with blue flowers.

"You looks ever so lovely, Miss!" the maid said as if she had asked the question.

"Thank you, Ethel," Luella replied.

As she reached the top of the stairs, she saw that the Duke was waiting for her in the hall. It was with the utmost difficulty that she managed to walk down them slowly. She wanted desperately to run and be with him. He was looking exceedingly smart and more handsome than ever.

"I must commend you on being so punctual," he said. While he spoke conventionally, his eyes were saying things which made her heart beat furiously. He seemed to take her breath away.

The carriage was waiting outside and to her surprise the Duke was not driving it. There were a coachman and a footman on the box. The butler and six footmen saw them off. Luella was aware that there was a brake behind to carry the luggage. The servants bowed as they drove off.

The Duke took Luella's hand. "You are very beautiful, my darling," he said softly.

"Th . . that is . . what I want . . you to think,"

Luella replied in a whisper. It was somehow difficult to speak. Her love for him seemed to be surging up inside her.

They drove down Park Lane. When they reached the end of it they turned to the right with the wall of the garden of Buckingham Palace on their left. "Where . . are we . . going?" she asked. "This . . is not . . the way to . . the Castle."

"I had a better idea during the night," the Duke said, "and I am hoping, my precious, it is something of which you will approve."

Luella wanted to say she would approve of anything as long as she could be with him. But she thought it would be a mistake. "I ought . . not to be . . here," she told herself. "I should have . . said goodbye and . . left him. It will only . . make things . . worse when the . . moment comes and I could not . . bear him to be . . unhappy."

Almost as if he knew what she was thinking, the Duke took her hand, lifted it to his lips and kissed it. "Stop worrying and leave everything to me," he said.

Luella looked up at him. Then because he was looking down at her it was impossible to look away. She was suddenly aware that the carriage had come to a standstill. She found to her surprise that they were on the Embankment beside the Thames. "Why are we . . here?" she asked.

"I have something to show you," the Duke answered. He helped her out of the carriage. As they started to walk she saw a little way ahead of them there was a large, important-looking yacht.

Before she could ask any questions the Duke was helping her up the gangway. They were piped aboard with the Captain and two junior officers receiving them. "It is a great honour to have you aboard, Your Grace," the Captain said.

"I am delighted to be here," the Duke replied, "and I wish to put to sea immediately."

"That is what I expected Your Grace to say," the Captain smiled.

Bewildered, Luella allowed the Duke to take her across the deck. They went into what she found was a beautifully decorated saloon. When he shut the door behind them she said in a very small voice: "What is .. h.happening? Wh.What are .. we doing?"

"We are eloping!" the Duke said. "When you told me about your father, my darling, I knew exactly what I should do. We are running away, just as your mother and father did!"

"But .. you cannot .. y. you .. must not .. !" Luella started to protest.

"When you left me," the Duke said, "I asked myself whether I was a man or a mouse. Then I had the answer – I was a duke – and dukes can do things that ordinary people cannot do."

He gave a short laugh as he said: "When we come home after a very long honeymoon, I can assure you that as a royal-blooded Duchess you will be received by my family with open arms."

"B.but .. the Queen .. what will .. the Queen say?" Luella asked in a whisper.

"It was very unfortunate, but I left for my honeymoon before I could open the Queen's letter inviting me – or *ordering* me, whichever you like – to Windsor Castle."

Because she could not help it, Luella laughed. "Oh, darling, darling!" she exclaimed. "How can you . . do anything so . . outrageous?"

"We will be married as soon as we have put out to sea, just as your father and mother were," the Duke said. "Now the world is at your feet, and you can choose where we will go."

Luella could only stare at him, thinking this could not be true. "Personally," the Duke said, "I think we should start in Greece. It was the story of your father's elopement which made me remember this yacht, which belonged to my cousin, the Marquess of Gates." He paused a moment and then smiled before adding: "It is now mine and has just been renovated. I hope you appreciate all that has been done."

"Do you . . really mean that . . we can be . . married?" Luella asked.

The engines were already throbbing under their feet. "There is no escape now," the Duke replied. "Aunt Anne would say I have definitely compromised you!"

Luella tried to laugh, but his arms were round her and his lips were on hers.

It was very late that night when Luella stirred against her husband's shoulder. "Are you awake, my precious?" he asked.

"How can I sleep when I am . . so happy?" Luella replied. "Even now I cannot . . believe I am . . really your . . wife . . and I do not have to l.leave you."

"I would never have let you leave me," the Duke said, "and it was very wrong and unkind of you to try."

"I .. I was .. only thinking .. of you . . ."

"I know that, my lovely one," the Duke said, "and that is something you will now have to do for the rest of your life."

Luella gave a little cry. "It is .. like a fairytale! I am .. so happy I cannot .. believe I am not .. dreaming!"

"We will dream together," the Duke said, "and if you are happy, my adorable wife, I can assure you I am the luckiest man in the world to have found you!"

"I love you .. I love you .. I love you!" Luella cried, pressing her lips against his shoulder.

The Duke pulled her closer still so that she could feel his heart beating against hers. "You are the wife I have always wanted, but thought I would never find," he said tenderly.

"And you .. are the star .. I thought was .. out of reach," Luella whispered.

The Duke turned to find her lips. She could feel his hand touching her body and knew she had not only touched the stars. They were now in their hearts, their minds and their souls.

They were theirs for all Eternity.